THE SECRET OF
BUNRATTY CASTLE

W9-CPC-160

*For Darrin,
my very best Burton beach buddy,
with love.*

CONTENTS

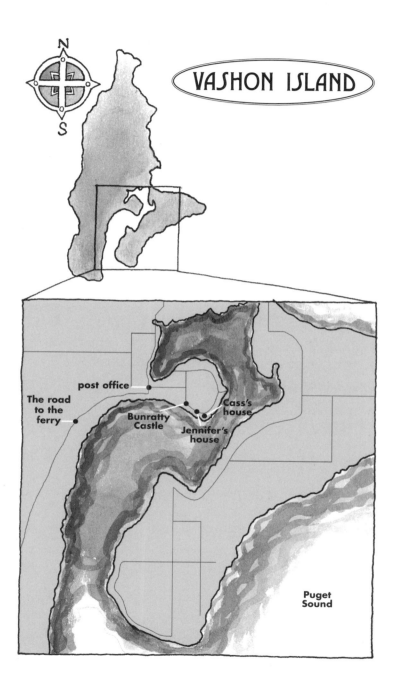

N

S

VASHON ISLAND

post office

The road
to the
ferry

Bunratty
Castle

Jennifer's
house

Cass's
house

Puget
Sound

CHAPTER 1 ✿ SUMMER PEOPLE

It was summer, the very ripest part of summer when the trees were thick with leaves, the flowers bloomed in the park, and the sun sat high in a wide clear-blue sky. The bay was even deeper blue than the sky, and from the back seat, Jennifer Chang could see the seagulls circling over the dock as her mother eased the station wagon down the ramp and onto the ferryboat as it pulled against its lines.

Because it was the first Saturday of summer vacation, the ferry was crowded with cars filled with families and dogs and cats and beach gear and clothes and groceries. From below the deck, the ferry's engine rumbled to life. The noise throbbed in Jennifer's head but was not loud enough to drown out Margo's voice from the seat beside her.

"Oh, Mom. Oh, Dad. How *could* you?"

Mr. Chang, a good-natured man whose favorite pastime was piecing together jigsaw puzzles, turned his head and answered his older daughter. "How could we what?"

"You know what, Dad," Margo huffed, dramatically tossing her shiny black hair over her shoulders. "Drag us away from our home and our friends. Carry us off to some deserted island for the whole summer. It just isn't fair!" Margo sank down in the seat, folding her arms across her chest, sulking in stubborn silence.

Mrs. Chang, wearing her favorite pair of purple overalls, shut off the engine and looked over her shoulder. "You'll love the island, honey. You both will."

"Rrreow."

"Was that you, Margo?" Mrs. Chang asked.

"No, Mom. That was Fat Cat. He doesn't want to go either," Margo replied firmly. She poked her finger through the wire mesh of her cat's carrier and stroked his nose.

For the past two weeks, Jennifer had been listening to her fifteen-year-old sister complain. It had started the day her parents announced they had bought a beach house on Vashon Island where the family would be spending their summer vacations each year when school got out.

"Our house is a real old charmer," Mr. Chang had assured them. "Built in 1906 by Odelia and Jasper Adams of Burton beach, it sits on a hill just a hop, skip, and a jump from a beautiful sandy beach. At least, that's what the real estate agent told us – your mom and I didn't have a chance to see the beach. There's even room at the house for your mother's pottery gear. You two girls can really have a ball on the beach. And I'll be able to commute to my office in Seattle on the morning ferry. It's perfect."

But Margo had wished she could have stayed in Seattle to be near her friends and to play on her new summer-league soccer team.

"You'll make new friends," her mother had explained. "There are lots of families that spend the summer on Vashon. You'll be able to go swimming and boating and fishing."

"I get seasick in boats," Margo had complained. "And fish are stinky."

To Jennifer, who was three years younger than her sister, the idea of spending the summer on an island sounded more appealing than playing games on the city pavement or swimming in the crowded public pool. This summer there would be swimming in the salt water of the Puget Sound.

Jennifer knew this summer was going to be different. Special. She rolled down the window. Fresh gusts of salt air swept up her braids. Behind the ferry she watched as the Seattle skyline shrank away. Looking ahead, she felt a tingle of excitement as the island, green with towering pine trees, came into view.

As the ferry bumped the dock, its engine quieted to a purr. Mrs. Chang started the car and steered it carefully up the ramp.

As the car sped along, Jennifer settled back and looked out the window. She saw that the island was mostly trees and fields full of blackberry vines and apple orchards. Every now and then they passed a house. The island houses were more rustic, Jennifer thought, than those in Seattle where she had grown up.

The road dropped down and followed the edge of the water. There were more houses now. Jennifer noticed some were boarded up. Perhaps they belonged to people like her own family who stayed on the island for summers only. Some of the houses had poles set out in the water. Pulley ropes ran from the poles up to the bulkhead: the wall in the water built to protect the shore from the waves. Boats bobbed at these ropes waiting to be pulled ashore for fishing or waterskiing.

Across the water the island curved around, and Jennifer could see what must be farms and orchards on its far side. The tide was all the way up now. She would have to wait until evening to see what the beach looked like. Jennifer was so intent on the scenery that she hardly noticed the ridge of clouds creeping up from the horizon.

Mr. Chang tapped on the window as the car slowed to turn a sharp corner. "This is the town of Burton. It's very small: just a store, gas station, and post office. A little ways down the beach is our house," he boasted. They passed the post office and a corner store. "In the old days," he explained, "a dirt road followed the beach. That's closed off to traffic now. We take that road up the hill and double back.

The car climbed a hill and then slowed at a driveway canopied by branches. The name Adams was chipping off a sign nailed to a tree trunk. Mrs. Chang turned in. Gravel crunched under the tires as the car bounded in and out of ruts and came to a stop by a dilapidated garage, leaning to one side. It looked as though it was on the brink of total collapse. One good storm and it would surely tumble right down the hillside.

"Here it is," Mr. Chang announced. "Home sweet home."

Everyone piled out of the car and looked down the hill to the house below.

"Isn't it simply magnificent?" grinned Jennifer's father.

"It positively oozes with charm!" cried Mrs. Chang. "And that porch is definitely perfect for my pottery wheel."

"Just look at how big it is," Jennifer added in awe. "And there are so many trees. It's great. It's terrific."

"It's a dump," Margo mumbled, staring in dismay at the drab gray house that waited under the shadows of the pine trees. She looked at the

trees and hills all around. "And I bet there's no flat place to practice soccer."

Ignoring Margo's remarks, Mr. Chang opened the back of the station wagon. "Everyone grab a box. We'll get settled in and have a fantastic celebration dinner."

Clutching boxes of food and bags of clothing, they followed the path that zigzagged down the hill to the house. Unlike their yard at home, which was trimmed with rosebushes and kept neatly mowed, the hillside was wild with wandering weeds and full of bushes and ivy that climbed right up the thick trunks of the pine trees. Here and there ferns grew in patches of daylight as did a plant with red wrinkled leaves that Jennifer had never seen before.

The trail was covered with layers of decaying leaves and pine needles. Somewhere above, an animal startled by the newcomers shrieked and dropped a pinecone. It bounced off Margo's head, and she stumbled over a root, stubbing her toe on it. "Ouch! I told you this place was full of mountains," Margo shouted, jumping back. "I'll break my leg before I have a chance to get a soccer ball out of the box."

"That mountain," Mrs. Chang laughed, giving Margo a friendly grin, "was a tree root. Now keep moving, this box is heavy. What's in it anyway?"

"Oh," Margo sighed. "That's my soccer book and magazine stash. I couldn't survive out here without them. I hope I remembered to have my magazine subscriptions forwarded!"

A light drizzle was beginning to fall as Mr. Chang stretched out from under his backpack full of fishing gear and unlocked the front door of the big house.

They stepped inside. It was damp and dark and very still.

"I'll open the curtains," Mrs. Chang said, setting her box on the floor. She groped her way through the darkness. "Ow!"

"What's wrong, Mom?" Margo gasped.

"Now it's my turn. I stubbed my toe on something. Don't worry, I'm fine. I'll have to get used to bumping into things in this old house!"

A moment later the curtains were swept back and suddenly the room was alive with furniture, all of it old. Tables with heavy carved legs (like the one Mrs. Chang had stubbed her toe on) and chairs with curving backs and worn velvet cushions that might once have been maroon, greeted them. Jennifer's feet sank into the rug that swirled with flowers, faded now, but somehow nicer that way.

Light filtered in through a row of windows that looked out over Quartermaster Harbor and across to the fishing boats moored at Dockton. Along the opposite wall stood a fireplace, black with age. On the mantel sat a cast-iron dog. Jennifer discovered that when she lifted the dog's tail, its jaws popped open.

"It's a nutcracker," Mr. Chang explained. "My Uncle Ed used to have one. I remember it well. I knocked it on his foot when I was six years old."

"Oh, Dad, you did not!" Jennifer giggled.

"Indeed I did. Uncle Ed couldn't walk for a week. He never let me forget that!"

Everyone laughed except Margo, who was still standing in the middle of the room surveying the furniture with disbelief. "This is not a house," she said, staring at a huge vase painted with camels and elephants. "It's a museum. Yuck. And where is the TV? How can I keep up with the World Cup tournament? It only comes once every four years!" She dumped a box of towels on the couch and stalked out of the room.

Jennifer's eyes traveled from the sofa to the footstool, which after years of use looked more like a mushroom, to the collection of ornate dishes in a glass cabinet, to the paintings of old sailing ships that lined the walls.

The kitchen, she discovered, though equally as ancient as the living room, seemed bare in comparison. The walls were painted a soft buttery yellow, and the sink was deep and darkened with age. At one end, a rusted pump with a curved handle stood like a soldier at attention. The floorboards, polished smooth by decades of use, creaked under Jennifer's feet. By far the most striking object was the refrigerator. It was so old that its motor sat on top of it like a beehive. It hummed like a beehive too when Mrs. Chang flicked the switch in the fuse box. An aroma of cinnamon and wood hung in the air, and soft lights made everything glow warmly.

"This place oozes with charm," Mrs. Chang repeated over and over as she examined the dusty wood-burning stove and the array of pots and pans that hung above it, neatly covered in cobwebs.

"Hey, check this out," Margo called from the room at the bottom of the stairs. It was the bathroom, and Margo was twirling the taps on an ancient bathtub. It had a sloped back, curving sides, and stood on four clawed feet painted gold.

"What a tub!" Margo cried. "Perfect for a long bath after a hard workout." She turned off the water and grinned. "Maybe living in a museum isn't so bad after all." She jumped up, then pounded up the stairs to see the bedrooms.

Jennifer climbed back up the path to the car and carried Fat Cat's box back down, setting it on the porch. The porch stretched around three sides of the house, and from the front she could see the whole harbor, still gray with rain. Overhead in the branches a squirrel chattered, and the air was sweet with the scent of pine needles.

Jennifer was feeling as carefree as a bird when suddenly she heard a door inside slam and Margo's voice burst out, "Mom! You never said when we moved out here that I would have to share a room."

"Sorry, honey. But there are only two bedrooms here. We originally thought that a house this size would have at least three. There's nothing we can do about it."

"Oh, Mom."

Jennifer leaned against the railing. She did not want to be part of the argument. Even though Margo had a few strange habits like doing leg lifts every night, she was a nice sister most of the time. She even helped Jennifer with her math. But when it came to sharing a room, Margo was very opinionated. *Very.* Jennifer knew how she felt. Sometimes she liked to be alone too. Sharing a room with a sister, which they did back in Seattle, made that hard to do.

"No offense to Jennifer," Margo was saying, "but I wouldn't even want to share a room with the Queen of Sheba."

"Hey everybody, come and look at this," Mr. Chang called to them from the steps of an old shed built next to the kitchen.

"Not now, " Mrs. Chang answered through the window. "I'm trying to solve this problem."

"I know. I've heard," Mr. Chang replied. "But I think it's solved already. Come and see."

CHAPTER 2 ❧ COME BACK, FAT CAT

Jennifer, Margo, and the girls' mom joined Mr. Chang at the shed door. They peered inside. A shaft of daylight managed to struggle through the grimy windows, revealing a large shadowy room cluttered with old chests, broken furniture, and junk stacked halfway to the rafters. By the looks of it, the shed had been used as a storeroom for many years.

"A junk room. So what?" Margo said.

"Don't you see?" Mr. Chang smiled and pointed inside. "Under those steamer trunks is a bed, a brass bed by the looks of it. Back behind that pile of boxes is a closet. In the old days this shed was a guest cottage or bunkhouse of sorts. That's why it has windows. With a little elbow grease, it could be fixed up again."

Margo's eyes grew narrow. "Oh, gross, Dad," she said, looking up at her father suspiciously. "There's no way I'm sleeping in this place!"

Jennifer looked around. Her father was right. Without the mountain of junk and with curtains hanging over the windows and a bit of polish applied to the brass bed, the room had definite potential. In fact, with Jennifer's posters (which Margo refused to let her hang up in their room at

home) hiding the bare board walls, and a rug covering the planks on the floor, the bunkhouse could be transformed into a real bedroom, a place of her own.

"I think it's neat," Jennifer spoke up.

"You like it?" Margo stared at her sister in amazement.

"Yes. I could throw out the junk and clean it up just fine," Jennifer said, eagerly.

"I'll be glad to make some curtains," Margo volunteered. If it meant getting her own room, she was happy to help, even if it involved sewing.

"Are you sure you won't mind sleeping out here alone?" Mrs. Chang asked. "It'll get *very* dark."

Everyone in the family knew Jennifer didn't like dark places. Although she never said so, she worried that something was hiding in the dark waiting to jump out and grab her. Jennifer didn't even like going into a closet unless the light was on. "You're such a fraidy-cat," Margo would tease. "Even Fat Cat is braver than you!"

"I'll be fine," Jennifer argued. "Really, I will. The house is only ten feet away."

"I suppose it would be all right," Mrs. Chang agreed, looking at her husband.

"I think Jennifer is old enough to take care of her own bunkhouse this summer," Mr. Chang added.

"Good," said Jennifer, hugging her parents.

"Good," echoed Margo with relief.

"May I stay here and get started?" Jennifer asked with excitement.

Her father nodded. "We can finish unloading the car without you." He crossed over to the porch and slid the pack with its fishing gear on a bench. He pointed to Fat Cat's carrier. "You can take care of the cat. Too big a chance he'll slip out the door with us going in and out," he said. Jennifer heard growls coming from Fat Cat's direction.

"Cats have to stay inside three days after moving," Mrs. Chang explained. "So whatever you do, don't let Fat Cat outside. He'll get lost!"

Jennifer stepped into the bunkhouse kicking the door shut behind her. She set Fat Cat's box on the floor. Unhooking the latch, she lifted the lid. A very plump, very angry orange cat exploded out of the box, his collar bell tinkling furiously. Realizing he was somewhere new, his curiosity won out over his anger and the cat began to sniff about, flicking his tail in disapproval.

Jennifer left Fat Cat to explore. Wading to the middle of the room, she stood knee-deep in the midst of dusty trunks, pillows, boxes of magazines, books, pictures, rusty machinery, and an assortment of ancient odds and ends. The best way to start, she decided, was to push everything into one heap in the center of the room. From there she could sort things out, one at a time, into various piles according to their value.

She began by shoving the trunks and a big green-and-white striped hatbox tied with a velvet ribbon across the floor. The handles of all three, she noticed, were engraved with the initials *I. A.*

Behind her, the door to the bunkhouse suddenly creaked. Jennifer spun around in time to see Fat Cat slipping outside.

"Come back, Fat Cat!" she cried, scrambling to the door. "Come back!" A flash of orange streaked into the bushes beyond the porch. Jennifer followed. "Here kitty, kitty, kitty. Come here," Jennifer called, crawling along on her hands and knees in the wet leaves. She hoped to hear the tinkling of Fat Cat's collar bell. But all she heard were the last few drops of rain pattering through the trees.

It was impossible to see into the heavy undergrowth. "Come back, Fat Cat," she called over and over again, the words of her mother echoing in her ear. "Whatever you do, don't let Fat Cat outside. He'll get lost. He'll get *lost.*"

Jennifer had to find him. It would be dark soon. Then he'd be lost for sure. She felt like crying, when suddenly Fat Cat shot across the path toward the house next door.

Blackberry vines along the path scratched at her legs. Once she was through the path, Jennifer was disappointed to see the porch of the white house empty. Fat Cat was gone.

Panic rose up inside her. "If I have to search all night, I'll find that cat."

She noticed another path, not at all overgrown, leading from the porch down toward the water. Maybe Fat Cat had followed it. Jennifer hurried down to a dirt road that ran beside the bulkhead. A boathouse stood above the water. A small red boat with an outboard motor on it tugged at its line from the rickety dock that extended out in front into the water.

Jennifer looked up and down the road but saw no sign of the orange cat. She couldn't imagine that Fat Cat would head for the beach. He hated water. Leaning over the wooden boards of the bulkhead, Jennifer got another surprise. Instead of the sandy beach her father had described, she saw rocks and bricks covered with barnacles and seaweed. A row of pebbles pushed up by waves was the only place to walk on the beach.

"Sandy, my foot," grumbled Jennifer in dismay.

"Sandy Krewson, to be exact," a voice behind her snapped.

Jennifer spun around. A girl her age with frizzy fox-red hair and a million freckles stood on the

rocks at the end of the path. In her arms a squirming orange cat tried determinedly to free itself. Jennifer breathed a huge sigh of relief.

"I believe this bundle of claws is yours." The girl opened her arms. Fat Cat leaped to the ground and before he could slip away, Jennifer scooped up her sister's cat.

"Thanks a million," Jennifer said, soothing the frustrated animal. "Where did you find him?"

"He found me," the girl explained and shoved her hands in the pockets of her jeans. "One minute I was filling the birdbath, and the next thing I knew, this orange fluffball jumped into my arms. Then you came tearing through the bushes and ran down our trail."

The girl gave Jennifer a suspicious look. "Just how did you know my name was Sandy anyway? Are you a mind reader?"

Jennifer giggled. "I didn't. I said 'sandy' when I saw the beach. My dad told me it was a sandy beach. But it's not. It's rocky and awful."

"My dad exaggerates too, especially when he tells me how many thousands of fish the crew on his boat is catching up in Alaska each summer." The girl laughed to herself, then said, "By the way, do me a favor. Call me Cass instead of Cassandra or Sandy, OK?"

"Sure," Jennifer agreed and sat down on the bulkhead petting Fat Cat, who began to purr like a lawn mower. Cass came and sat down next to her and dangled her feet over the side. For a moment she studied the hole in the toe of her sneaker. Then she slapped her knee. "Hey," she cried and looked at Jennifer. "You must be the summer people who bought the old Adams place."

"Old is right," Jennifer nodded. "My sister calls it a museum."

"There are plenty of houses older than yours on this island," Cass assured her. "Bunratty Castle, for example."

"Why did you call us 'summer people'?" Jennifer asked. "And what is Bunratty Castle?"

Cass pushed a handful of hair out of her face and said, "On Vashon Island you either live here year-round and are an islander, or you come out for the summer, lap up the sun, and then go back to the city before the stormy weather begins."

"That's exactly what we're doing," Jennifer said. She was surprised her neighbor knew so much about her family without knowing them at all.

"Then you are summer people. A different group altogether." Cass paused to scratch Fat Cat's chin. "As for Bunratty Castle," she continued, "it's just down the road."

Cass stood up and dusted off her jeans. "You'd better get your cat home before he gets away again. He'll probably be scared of the raccoons, you know."

"I didn't know there were raccoons here," Jennifer said, trying her best to be friendly.

"Summer people, all right," Cass said spinning around. "I'd better go. My mom's a real worrywart while my dad is away." She started up the trail then stopped. "Why don't you come over tomorrow? I'll show you my collection of postcards from Alaska."

Jennifer's heart skipped. "OK," she answered.

"Great," Cass called over her shoulder. "I'll see ya later, alligator."

"After a while, crocodile," Jennifer called back. But Cass, her hair waving like a red flag, was already gone.

CHAPTER 3 ❀ THE TREAJURE HUNT

Because Jennifer's parents had successfully filled the kitchen with smoke while attempting to get a fire lighted in the wood-burning stove, the family sat down to a dinner of cold baked beans and salad.

"It tickles my funny bone to be sitting at this elegant old table eating beans," Mr. Chang grinned good-naturedly.

"I wonder how people used to make that stove work?" Mrs. Chang puzzled, scraping beans from a can onto Margo's plate.

"Those folks probably used *dry* wood," Mr. Chang said with a hint of amusement in his voice.

"And that pump at the sink, I thought my arm would fall off before the rusty water turned clear. How long do you suppose it has been since all this stuff was used?" She passed the plate to her husband.

"The Adams moved out years ago. The place has been closed up ever since," Mr. Chang said, setting the plate before Margo. "It could be the stovepipe is jammed with leaves. We'll check it tomorrow."

"Do we really have to eat this?" Margo whimpered. She stared painfully at her plate. "Don't we have potato chips or anything good to eat? I need *something* to keep me going."

"One night of beans won't hurt you, honey," Mrs. Chang said. "It might even be good for you."

"It's this or cat food," Mr. Chang teased.

"Oh, Dad," Margo winced. "Right." She stomped into the kitchen for the salad bowl.

"This reminds me of camping," Jennifer said. "Especially because it's raining outside."

"Outside is not the only place it's raining," Margo announced from the doorway, where she watched two drops of water fall from the kitchen ceiling onto her plate. "I knew this place would leak," she said, plopping herself down at the table.

Without a word, Mrs. Chang got up and strategically placed a bucket on the floor to catch both drips at once. She sat down and looked at Jennifer. "I think you should sleep in here tonight. No telling how leaky that bunkhouse roof may be."

Jennifer agreed. Without having to explain that she hadn't even started the cleanup, she gladly unrolled her sleeping bag on the carpet by the fireplace after dinner.

All night it poured down rain, but Jennifer did not mind. She camped out on the floor, Fat Cat purring at her side.

As she slept, she dreamed of finding hidden treasure buried in the bunkhouse. She'd open a hatbox and there would be gems. She'd lift the lid of a trunk and discover it to be full of gold coins. Under the bed were bundles of money, and in the corners were piles of priceless jewelry.

She was still thinking about treasure as she excused herself from the breakfast table the next morning. She was in a hurry to start cleaning the bunkhouse and to see what she could find.

The rain continued pelting down, falling in big drops from the branches onto Jennifer's head as she raced across the yard and up the bunkhouse steps. Inside she listened to the rain drumming on the roof like a thousand fingers.

Jennifer surveyed the room. It was hard to decide just where to start the cleanup. First she tried sweeping. But every time she shifted a box or lifted a load of clothes, another explosion of dust and dried moths wings swirled around the floor.

Sorting out the valuable objects from the junk would be a better idea, Jennifer decided. She could clean later. But this was not nearly as easy or as fun a job as she'd imagined. Most of the boxes were crammed with broken bits of china, old rags that smelled of mildew, and crumbling books. Once she thought she'd discovered a valuable painting only to have it disintegrate between her fingers.

After two hours of finding more moth-eaten clothes, more rusted tools, more broken dishes, more magazines green with mold, and more useless junk, Jennifer heaved herself up and wiped her dirty face on her dirty sleeve. Her eyes stung with grit, and her knees were aching from crawling on the hard floor.

To make matters worse, she'd found nothing more valuable than a toothbrush with an ivory handle, and the bunkhouse looked worse now than when she had started.

Jennifer was considering calling it quits for the day when the door creaked open behind her. Cass stepped in. Sweeping back the hood of her sweatshirt, she brushed the rain from her shoulders and gave her head a shake. She looked around at the mess.

"What are you doing? Trying to get in the book of records for the world's biggest junk collection?"

"I'm actually cleaning this place up," Jennifer replied, wiping the dirt from her eyes. "Trying to, anyway. Only it's a lot more work than I thought."

Cass looked surprised. "What on earth for? Do you have a passion for cleaning disaster areas, or are you just cuckoo? I mean this place is terminally dirty. You could disappear in here and never be found again."

Jennifer frowned. "My parents said I could have the bunkhouse for a bedroom this summer *if* I got it cleaned up."

"A whole bunkhouse to yourself!" Cass gasped.

Jennifer nodded happily and used her jeans to wipe the grime off her hands. "I was hoping to discover some treasure in here. But as you see, so far it's just trash."

"And plenty of it," Cass observed with a snicker. "Aren't you even going to ask me to help? We can look at my postcards another day."

"Would you help?"

"Sure," Cass replied. "Not only am I the world's quickest and best cleaner, but I am a certified A-number-one snoop as well."

All afternoon, as the rain beat at the windows, Cass and Jennifer worked, sweeping up clouds of dust, shoving boxes from one corner to another, and using a mop to swipe cobwebs from the rafters.

It was when Cass opened the window to shake out the duster that she knocked a wasp nest off the sill. "Yikes!" she cried, leaping back. "I'm glad there are no wasps still living in here."

Cass picked up the nest gingerly and gave it a shake. "Is it OK if I give this to my brother? Paul collects nature stuff like this. His shelves are full of dried-up bird nests and feathers and rocks."

Jennifer agreed, and when they'd finished scrubbing the windows and floor and trudging up the hill carrying load after load of trash to the garbage cans, they finally flopped down on the floor to rummage through the last few boxes they had turned upside down in the middle of the room.

Right away Cass uncovered a set of strange old-fashioned ladies underwear that she swore looked like her gym clothes from school. She also found a lopsided gray flannel hat with a broken feather and two dresses perfect for masquerade parties. In the closet, Jennifer discovered a radio the size of a breadbox. It was so old it had tubes that crackled and popped when she plugged it in. After a moment of suspense, a Seattle radio station came in through the static so the girls had music to listen to as they continued the search for treasure.

It was at the very bottom of a box that Jennifer uncovered a photograph album and several Vashon Island newspapers yellow with age. The rain beat steadily on the bunkhouse windows as Jennifer thumbed through a paper so old that its edges were brown and the paper cracked as she turned the page.

The headlines on one paper dated May 12, 1921, jumped out at her. "Belle of Burton Beach Enters Society."

"Hey, Cass, listen to this. 'Miss Isabelle Adams, niece of Odelia and Jasper Adams of Burton beach, celebrated her eighteenth birthday today at the gracious home of her aunt and uncle.' That must be our house," Jennifer smiled and continued. "'The debutante, raised since childhood by her loving aunt and uncle was presented to society with a bouquet of roses as well as...'"

"As well as what?" Cass asked, shaking out another bunch of dusty old rags.

"I can't tell," Jennifer squinted. "The rest of the article is too moldy to read. But look at this picture." She handed the paper to Cass.

The photograph was clear. It showed Isabelle standing solemnly on the front porch of the beach house between a severe looking older lady, who the girls guessed was Aunt Odelia, and a tall gray-haired man with an Abraham Lincoln beard, who must have been Uncle Jasper.

Jennifer and Cass stared at the photograph. "Isabelle Adams," Jennifer murmured. "Isabelle Adams. *I. A.* These trunks in the corner must have belonged to her!" Jennifer cried. "They have the initials *I. A.* engraved on the handles."

"Oooh, this gives me goose bumps," Cass shivered. "It's weird knowing all this stuff belonged to those people. Do you suppose their ghosts are hanging over our heads watching us?"

Suddenly, before Jennifer could answer, the radio crackled as if it had been hit by lightning. Jennifer jumped. "Don't be silly, Cass," she said in an unsteady voice. "There's no such thing as ghosts. I'm sure."

"How exactly do you know that?" Cass asked suspiciously.

"I just do, that's all," Jennifer replied nervously, yanking an old apron out from between two books. As she did, something flew out of the pocket and rolled under the bed.

Jennifer lay down on her stomach and stretched her arm under the bed as far as it would go. "Crumbs," she grimaced. "We forgot to sweep under here." Her hand swept back and forth, finally brushing against a marble-sized object. She grasped it and sat up.

Opening her hand she stared in disbelief. "It's an earring," she cried, rolling it over in her hand. It was a blood-red stone as clear as crystal set in a cluster of what looked to be diamond chips.

"Is it a real ruby?" Cass asked.

"I hope so," Jennifer replied. She passed the earring to Cass, and as she did, something shiny in the rafters caught her eye.

"What's that?" Jennifer stood up, pointing to the beam that ran across the center of the bunkhouse.

Cass glanced up. "It's a cobwebby old beam full of bugs," she replied and went back to studying the earring.

"No, Cass. Look closer. There's definitely something up there." Using the mop to brush the cobwebs away, Jennifer climbed up on a box and lifted a metal object off a nail in the beam. She held it in her hand a moment, looking at it.

"It's a key," Jennifer exclaimed.

"A key," Cass repeated. "What's it doing way up there?"

Jennifer climbed down and inspected the key closely. It was discolored with age and much larger than other keys she had seen. Shaped like an old-fashioned key, it had two prongs sticking out at the bottom and a hole at the base where it had been hung over the nail. Although worn, the body of the key was engraved with a swirl of flowers Jennifer guessed were roses.

"What kind of key is it?" Cass asked.

"Beats me," replied Jennifer. "It looks more like a skeleton's arm than a key. It's heavy too."

"See if it fits in the door," Cass suggested.

But the key was too fat to fit in the lock of the bunkhouse door. So Jennifer unfastened the clasp on her necklace and threaded it through the hole in the key.

"Hey, Jennifer, that looks neat. The *ssseeecret* key necklace," Cass said in her spooky voice.

Jennifer tucked the key inside her sweater. It felt cold against her skin. "I'll wear it for good luck," she grinned. "Maybe someday we'll find out what door this key opens."

"Maybe," yawned Cass. "Maybe not." She glanced at her watch. "Yikes, it's getting dark already. I'd better go or Paul will eat everything on the dinner table."

She got up and started for the door. "If it's nice tomorrow I'll give you a tour of the beautiful barnacled beach, OK?"

"Sure," Jennifer agreed. "And thanks for helping."

"See ya later, alligator," Cass smiled, flopping the hood of her sweatshirt over her head.

"After a while, crocodile," Jennifer answered. Grabbing the photograph albums and newspaper to show her family, she followed Cass outside.

Inside the house a blazing fire crackled and hissed with driftwood, casting a cheery glow around the living room. Most of the boxes were gone, but the kitchen counter was stacked with food and dishes. The sound of rock music drifted down from the radio upstairs.

Jennifer scraped her feet on the mat and stepped over the bucket that was still catching drips from the ceiling. "It sure is dark out there," she remarked to her mother. She set the photo albums on the counter and hung her sweater on a hook behind the door. "I'm glad the kitchen light was on or I'd have stepped in a giant puddle. My shoes would have been soaking wet!"

Jennifer's mother was standing on a chair stacking food containers into the cupboard above the sink. "No city lights out here at night," she said over her shoulder. "I'll give you a flashlight. We wouldn't want you getting lost in the dark."

Jennifer passed her mother a set of spice jars. "Where are Dad and Margo? Did they desert you?"

Mrs. Chang laughed. "Your father is in the living room starting a puzzle of Mount Rainier, and Margo is still arranging her room."

Just then a window slammed and Margo came pounding down the stairs. "Guess what? Guess what!" she cried, trying not to drop the hand weights she was lugging.

"Not another leak?" Mrs. Chang sighed.

"Better," said Margo, her eyes aglow. "Guess who I saw on the porch next door? A boy, kicking a soccer ball. And he's good!"

"What's going on?" Mr. Chang called from the living room. "A leak?"

"Another soccer player," said Margo. "I'm going upstairs to see if he comes outside again."

She thundered up the stairs two at a time.

"That must be Paul," Jennifer smiled.

Her mother looked puzzled. "Who's Paul?"

"Paul is Cass's brother – Cass is the girl who lives next door," Jennifer explained. "Looks like Paul plays soccer."

"You'll have to introduce him to Margo."

"I will," Jennifer promised. "Just as soon as her feet touch the ground again."

CHAPTER 4 🌹 BUNRATTY CASTLE

When all the clutter was removed and the yellow curtains – made by Margo, who was just learning to sew – were up, a clean bedspread was on the bed, and a salvaged rug with all the dust beaten out of it was spread across the floor, the bunkhouse was transformed into a cheerful bedroom. Jennifer was especially pleased with the bookshelf she'd built herself out of planks and bricks. Books on horses and dogs and how to care for them stood on the bottom shelf, and her collection of china animals decorated the top.

Jennifer stayed up late arranging her books and tacking her posters of dogs, cats, horses, and other animals all over the walls. Jennifer loved animals. When she was little she'd begged for a horse but couldn't have one because they lived in the city. For her last birthday she had pleaded for a dog. But Margo argued it would eat Fat Cat. And even worse, her parents thought she was too young for such a big responsibility, so she'd gotten a guppy instead. The guppy had disappeared after one week. Jennifer suspected it had ended up inside the always-hungry Fat Cat. "I'll be a veterinarian when I grow up," Jennifer promised herself, "and

I'll live out in the country where I can keep all the animals I want."

As she tacked up the final poster, Jennifer glanced outside. It had turned as dark as the inside of a stove. The moon wasn't up yet either. An uncomfortable feeling grew inside Jennifer as she closed the curtains and slipped into her nightgown.

Maybe I won't be afraid of the dark out here after all, she said to herself as she crawled under the covers. Maybe I'll sleep just fine. But the moment the light went out her fears came flooding back. Except for the pale squares of the windows, the room was pitch-black. The night was full of strange noises: things scraping against the window, an animal calling, and something on the roof that kept rustling around.

Jennifer curled up in a ball, pulling the covers over her head. That was worse. If something did open the door and sneak in, she wouldn't hear it in time to scream. How she wished that key had fit the lock.

Jennifer thought about leaving the light on, but her parents were sure to notice, and Margo would tease her for being such a chicken.

Deciding it was best to shove a brick left over from the bookcase behind the door, Jennifer swung her feet out of bed. She was just groping for a brick in the darkness when she heard it: a low growling right outside the door. Then a frightening hiss.

"Fat Cat," Jennifer gasped, opening the door just wide enough for the cat to slip in. "I might have known. You aren't supposed to be outside, you know."

Pushing the brick into place, she crawled into bed with Fat Cat purring at her side. "You're no watchdog," Jennifer whispered to the cat, "but I'm glad you're here."

For a moment, Jennifer listened to the cat's purring, then she drifted off to sleep.

The next morning Jennifer awoke to the sun streaming in the bunkhouse windows. Even the birds were singing about it. Good, thought Jennifer as her fears of the previous night faded away, a perfect day for exploring the beach.

Sliding out of bed Jennifer pulled on her shorts and shirt and stuffed her feet into a pair of sandals. Although she still had the hatbox left to sort through, she felt like getting out in the sunshine. She ran a comb through her hair, parting it down the back then twisting it into two neat braids. She opened the door and followed Fat Cat to the kitchen.

"Hi, sleepyhead," Cass said, pressing her nose against the screen on the kitchen door. "Are you ready for your grand tour?" Cass was wearing the same pink sweatshirt and old jeans, except today the jeans were rolled up.

"One more bite of toast and I'm ready," Jennifer said, chewing fast.

"Are you two heading toward the store?" Mrs. Chang called. Dressed in her purple overalls and waving a screwdriver, she appeared from the corner of the porch where she was trying to put her potters wheel together. "I don't think I'll get a chance to get to Burton today, or any day until I get this wheel reassembled."

Jennifer heard her mother sigh. "Why are these contraptions always so simple to take apart and so hard to put back together?" She smiled at Jennifer and Cass. "Anyway, please ask if they carry the city newspapers at the store."

"We'll ask," Jennifer promised and followed Cass. The smell of earth and forest mingled with the sharp scent of the beach as the girls hurried down the trail to the beach road.

"Attention all tourists. Our tour of Burton beach begins with this amazing view of Quartermaster Harbor," Cass began with a sweeping hand gesture. "Note the blue sky, blue water, and blue sailboat on your left. For a special added attraction we have a beautiful sandy beach cleverly disguised by a million, zillion barnacles."

"Let's go wading," Jennifer interrupted.

Kicking off their shoes, the girls climbed over the bulkhead and into the water that slapped up over the rocks below. Still holding its winter chill, the water made their feet ache at first. "Hey, my feet look green," Jennifer commented, wiggling her toes under the water. She could feel the pebbles shift as the waves rushed up and fell back again. Suddenly, something else moved. Something about the size of a matchbox was pushing against Jennifer's foot.

"Help!" shrieked Jennifer. "It's after me. It's trying to bite me," she wailed, and jumped right out of the water splashing Cass.

"What?" asked Cass.

"I don't know!" screamed Jennifer, looking around to see what it was.

"It was probably a crab," Cass suggested. "The way you screamed I thought it was a shark. Come on, my feet feel like ice cubes."

"I'm done wading," Jennifer agreed, climbing up over the bulkhead. "Besides, I want to see Bunratty Castle."

Cass looked surprised. "Are you sure you're brave enough?"

"Sure I'm sure," Jennifer lied. "Crabs are the only thing I'm afraid of."

The girls sat on the bulkhead, put on their shoes, and started down the road. After years of disuse, the beach road was no more than a wide dirt path with weeds growing up in patches and potholes full of mud. They had to watch where they stepped. Following the bulkhead in a curving line, the road went all the way to Burton. There it met up with the main highway that ran from the ferry dock at the south end of the island to the dock at the north end where Mr. Chang caught the ferry to Seattle.

As they walked, they passed houses built back in the trees. Mostly summer places, they had barbecue grills on their porches and bicycles and water skis and oars scattered in the front yards.

It was getting hot now, and the sun poured down on their backs. Cass pulled off her sweatshirt and tied it around her waist.

Halfway to Burton she twirled to a stop at a spot where the skeleton of an old rowboat leaned against a gatepost. On the gate itself a sign in freshly painted letters read No Trespassing.

"Ladies and gentlemen," Cass said, pointing through the trees, "the one, the only, the famous, Bunratty Castle!"

Jennifer stopped cold and drew in a breath of surprise. "I can see why they call it a castle," she murmured as she stared through the trees at what could have been a fairy-tale castle in miniature with its turret and porches and high windows. Once, Jennifer imagined, the house must have been very fancy with its pointed roof and graceful

wooden trim around the eaves and porch. But time and neglect had attacked the house, leaving the balconies sagging, the shutters hanging crooked, and most of the trim falling off.

The roof was bent like the back of an old horse, large holes spotted the walls, and all but a few of the uppermost windows were boarded over. Jennifer felt as if the windows in the highest tower room were watching them through mysterious dark eyes.

The first floor of the house was lost behind plants as the yard was now a tangle of weeds and wild grass. Bordering the yard, the hedges, once neatly trimmed, had grown as high as the porch and were bound up by rosebushes left unpruned for generations. A row of dead apple trees stood in the corner, raising crooked arms up from the waist-high grass. Here and there thistles sprang up, and ivy ran wild over everything. Over the years, morning glory vines had knitted themselves over the woodpile like blue-flowered shawls.

Behind the house was a pile of rubble that might once have been a stable, but it had been captured by the weeds long ago.

A blanket of bees hummed over the entire yard. From the gate, Jennifer could barely see a narrow footpath leading toward the house.

What Jennifer could see gave her a haunting and lonely feeling. The old house looked broken and weary with decay, as if it were ready to give up and crumble away. Strangely, there was something familiar about the place. More of a feeling than anything else. Perhaps just a lost memory, Jennifer thought, a wave of sadness sweeping over her.

"I can't see it very well, Cass. The yard is too overgrown," Jennifer heard herself saying. "Can we get closer?"

"Are you nuts?" Cass replied, planting her hands on her hips. "Do you want the mean old ghost of Abel Bunratty to reach out and grab you with skeleton hands?"

"W-what?" Jennifer stuttered.

"Honestly, you summer people don't know beans about this island."

Jennifer looked puzzled. "Cass, what are you talking about?"

"Oh, all right," Cass sighed. "I'll fill you in. But don't blame me for your nightmares!" She sank down in the weeds and selected a blade of grass to chew on. Leaning against the fence, she waited while Jennifer sprawled out beside her.

"Abel Bunratty," she began in a hushed voice, "was a crazy old man. *Really* crazy. He never talked to anybody, and he never set foot outside this gate. He built the castle by himself and lived there all alone for fifty years. It's really weird, isn't it, Jennifer?"

Jennifer stared up at the tower. "I wonder why he went to so much work to build a castle but didn't share it with anyone?"

"He wasn't entirely alone," Cass continued. "He had one hundred dogs running loose inside. Some people say he had treasure hidden away in there, so he kept the dogs to make sure nobody sneaked in and stole it." Cass brushed the hair from her face then looked hard at Jennifer. "The neighbors said they could hear him chasing those dogs up and down the tower stairs, yelling and cursing like a madman."

"A hundred dogs!" Jennifer looked surprised. "Wow, I'd be happy if I had just one dog. What happened to him?"

"That's a mystery. No one really knows for sure," Cass shrugged. "After a while the neighbors didn't hear him anymore. But they were too scared to go inside, so they called the police. When the police finally came to investigate, they found him up in the tower. Dead." Cass lowered her voice to a whisper. "The dogs had eaten him. Only his skeleton was left, still sitting all alone in a rocking chair."

Jennifer shuddered. "What happened to all of the dogs?"

Cass shook her head. "That's a mystery too. When the police came, the dogs were gone, all of them. It seemed as if they vanished into thin air.

But they say Abel Bunratty's ghost still seeks revenge on those dogs," Cass continued. "Sometimes, late at night, people say you can hear Abel's ghost chasing the dogs up and down the tower stairs."

Jennifer's eyes dropped. "What a sad story. I feel sorry for Abel Bunratty. Why do you think he was such a hermit?"

"Crazy. Wacko," Cass replied. She twirled her finger in circles next to her head.

Jennifer stood up and dusted herself off. She gazed at the empty house. "Do you suppose his ghost actually roams around in there?"

The words were barely out of her mouth when a sound, like nothing she had ever heard before, rose up from deep within the castle. The mournful wail, like the howling of a wild animal, grew louder and louder until it filled the air and went shooting through Jennifer's body like an electric shock.

Cass froze to the spot. "What's that?" she cried.

But Jennifer didn't answer. She was already racing down the road toward home.

CHAPTER 5 🌹 CHICKEN

"Wait! Wait for me!" Cass cried as she ran, finally catching up to Jennifer at the boat shed.

"Come on," Jennifer panted. "To the bunkhouse. Quick. If he saw us... he'll... get us!"

Jennifer fell on the slippery leaves as she sprinted up the trail, but no sooner had she landed than she was up and running again, the key bouncing around her neck. She didn't stop or look back until she'd slammed the door to the bunkhouse behind them.

For a moment there was silence. Jennifer felt her heart pounding in her chest. She slumped down on the hatbox, gasping to catch her breath. "Do you think... the ghost saw us?" she panted.

Cass, who had draped herself across the bed, was flushed from running. She nodded. "Why else do you think he screamed? I just hope he didn't follow us."

Then, from right outside, there came the sound of footsteps coming up the bunkhouse stairs. The door began to creak open. A shadow fell across the floor. The next thing the girls knew, two huge ghostly white hands reached around the door, slowly pushing it open.

"Ahhh!" screamed Cass, diving for the closet. "The ghost. Run! Run!"

But Jennifer did not budge. "That ghost," she grinned, "is my sister with her goalie gloves on."

Margo, decked out in full soccer uniform, stepped inside. "Mom wants to know if they have the city papers at Burton. Well? I don't have time to hang around here. I have to get ready."

"For what? The monsters' ball?" Jennifer replied, teasing her sister.

"Ha, ha, ha. It just so happens that boy next door – the only other soccer player on this big old island – is coming over to help Dad clean out the stovepipe, and I want to get psyched up for when I meet him. Anyway, let Mom know what you found out about the papers. I've got to go change before that boy gets here."

Again the bunkhouse door creaked opened. A long and thin shadow fell across the floor. All three girls jumped. "Hello. Anyone home? I'm supposed to help Mr.... Yikes! Who are you? The abominable snowgirl?" The teenage boy, who had rust-colored hair and a face full of freckles, took one look at Margo and jumped back with a big grin plastered on his face.

"That's no monster, Paul," Cass laughed from the corner. "That's Jennifer's sister."

Margo stood frozen like a statue, her mouth hanging wide open. "Oh, no," she said. Pushing past Paul, she bolted out the door, cleats clattering on the steps.

Paul watched her run around the corner of the porch. He shook his head. "That's some strange sister you've got there, Jennifer." And, by the way, thanks for the wasp nest. I keep it with my collection of petrified wood and fossilized fish."

"Sure thing," Jennifer smiled as Paul, still shaking his head, closed the door behind him.

"Let's go back," Cass blurted out.

"To the castle?" cried Jennifer in surprise. "No way. Never."

"But aren't you the least bit curious about who or what was howling?"

"Curious? Yes. Crazy? No," Jennifer stated. "Besides there's a No Trespassing sign. If someone saw us prowling around they might call the police."

Cass smiled slyly. "Not if we sneaked inside at night. Who knows, the ghost of Abel Bunratty might be hiding real treasure in the castle!"

"Sneak out at night when it's d-dark? You're crazy!" Jennifer stammered. "Besides, I am not allowed to sneak out."

"Who is?" Cass argued. "Why do you think it's called sneaking? Or maybe you're just a chicken? A little chicken from the city. Buk, buk, buk," Cass clucked and started flapping her arms energetically.

Jennifer felt a lump rising in her throat. If there was one person she never wanted to know about her fear of the dark, it was Cass. She swallowed the lump. "Of course I'm not scared," she lied. "But..."

"But what?"

"Oh, nothing," Jennifer sighed.

"Great," cried Cass. "We'll go tonight!"

"Tonight?" Jennifer looked shocked. "I still don't think it's such a smart idea..." she began. Just then a woman's voice called loudly, "Cassandra Amanda!"

"Oops, I'm late. I've got to go." Cass sprang to her feet. "I'll signal you at midnight by throwing a rock against your window. We'll meet down at the boat shed. Be ready and bring a flashlight."

The door slammed before Jennifer could utter a protest. In her heart she had a heavy feeling. Treasure or no treasure, sneaking down to Bunratty Castle did not sound safe, especially at night. And what if the ghost of Abel Bunratty still stalked in the darkness? Besides, her parents trusted her. If she got caught trespassing, it would be the end of her summer in the bunkhouse. And that was a chance she did not want to take.

CHAPTER 6 ❧ SNEAKING OUT

A summer wind rushed and swirled through the trees around the bunkhouse, keeping Jennifer's mind alert as she tossed and turned, trying to stay awake. All the lights in the house had gone out ages ago. Only the moon, nearly full, cast dancing shadows across the floor.

Jennifer rolled over for the umpteenth time, her mind skipping from the sound of the ghost's wailing cry to the prospect of uncovering hidden treasure inside the castle.

Would there be treasure chests or secret panels that would pop out of the wall to reveal diamonds, jewels, or priceless old coins? Who knows what crazy-man Bunratty might have stashed away all those years ago. And with someone brave like Cass along, what could go wrong?

Thoughts of treasure helped to melt the knot of anxiety in Jennifer's stomach. She was almost feeling excited about sneaking out when a stone cracked against the window. The hand of fear came rushing back and gripped her again. Her heart raced, her mouth went dry, and Jennifer nearly knocked the lamp off the table as she leaped out of bed.

Still dressed from that day, she had only to pull on her sneakers and grab the flashlight to go outside. Before opening the door, she tucked the key on her necklace inside her shirt, hoping it would indeed bring her good luck – at least help her stay alive.

The air was damp and heavy with the scent of pine needles, and Jennifer could just make out the top of the path beyond the porch. Under the kitchen windows, crickets chirped as Jennifer stepped forward reluctantly. Nothing would have made her happier than to turn around and climb back into the warmth and safety of her bed. But Cass would be waiting.

One step at a time Jennifer crept silently down the steps and past the kitchen windows. Skirting around the porch with its squeaking boards, Jennifer started down the trail, feeling her way with her feet.

Leaves crunched like cornflakes under her sneakers, making her wish she'd raked the path when her mother had asked her to. Farther now, she rounded the first bend, not daring to use the flashlight for fear her parents might choose that instant to look out the upstairs window.

As she neared the bottom of the hill, she could make out Cass's shadow by the boat shed.

"Pssst, over here, slowpoke," Cass whispered anxiously.

Breathing a sigh of relief, Jennifer suddenly felt adventurous. Perhaps they would find treasure in Bunratty Castle, or at least unravel the mystery of the howling voice.

The wind blew a sudden gust, wrinkling the water into an eerie black pattern. A mist was beginning to form.

"You took so long I thought you'd chickened out. Did you bring a flashlight?" Cass asked.

"Right here."

"Good. The batteries in mine were dead so we'll have to share. But don't turn it on yet. Come on."

Moonlight spilled over the treetops, throwing silvery blue shadows across the road. Everything, the trees, the houses, the bulkhead, even the boats at their moorings, took on the unreal glow of night.

Melting into the shadows at the side of the road, the girls walked in silence past darkened houses. For a moment Jennifer forgot it was nighttime. The moon balancing in the treetops sent its glow over the harbor. Insects hummed, and a gull circled the sky calling to its friend.

Then, all of a sudden, a dog heard their footsteps and came racing up, leaping at the fence in a frenzy of barking.

Crouching in grass, Jennifer and Cass didn't dare budge. Jennifer couldn't move, even to wipe away the spider web that draped across her neck. She prayed no spider was in it.

Both girls' legs felt cramped by the time the dog gave up its barking and trotted back to the porch with a final snort. They quickened their pace until they reached the gate.

Ahead of them Bunratty Castle loomed dark and sinister. It looked even more forbidding at night, as if the old house woke up to whisper secrets to the darkness. An eerie feeling swept through Jennifer again.

Cass glanced at her. "It's now or never," she whispered. She tugged at the gate until it creaked forward grudgingly. Cass stepped through, but Jennifer didn't follow at once, her mind stuck on the story of Abel Bunratty's ghost. She looked back down the road. It's not too late to turn back, she told herself. And it's definitely better to be a live chicken than a dead snoop.

"Come on," grumbled Cass over her shoulder. "Let's go!"

"Sorry," Jennifer apologized and started forward with a determined step.

"Go first," Cass whispered. "You've got the flashlight."

Jennifer stepped ahead and clicked on the flashlight, holding it low. Its beam made a bobbing path of light in the grass.

The pair steered a course among the tangle of weeds. In places, tangled vines blocked their way so completely that they had to rip their way through. Mosquitoes rose up and whined in their ears. Jennifer refused to look up at the house as they went for fear of what ghostly shape might be staring back.

By the time they were halfway, Jennifer had been bitten by a mosquito and had torn her sleeve on a thorn. Cass had just stumbled over a rock and stubbed her toe. Earwigs and spiders scuttled out of their way as the girls continued on. All around the yard, trees stood like giants, dark and swaying, watching everything.

The wind brushed Jennifer's face like a chilly finger, and all at once she had the feeling that something was looking down at them. She stopped in her tracks, her heart pounding in her throat. Without warning an owl swooped down uttering a mournful "Whooo?"

"I don't like this," Jennifer whispered. "It's getting really spooky."

"We're not even inside yet," Cass answered. "Go around to the back porch, or the neighbors might see our light."

"It's not the neighbors I'm worried about," Jennifer sighed.

Cass gave her a shove, and they moved cautiously past the rosebushes to the willow tree at the side of the house.

Jennifer kept thinking that at any moment someone or something was going to come screaming out the front door and grab them. She was relieved when they passed the willow and reached the back porch. Above their heads the dark tower of a house threatened, appearing to ripple as clouds rushed over its peaked roof. The girls waited a moment, each holding her breath and listening. All was silent.

Jennifer raised the light, shining it over the back of the house. Now that they were closer they could

see how broken down the old place was. Paint hung in strips from the weathered boards. The stairs leading up to the back porch sagged like a hammock. Several boards on the steps were missing. Jennifer pointed to them. Cass nodded.

Cautiously, the girls moved up the stairs one at a time. Jennifer did not dare look up until she'd crossed the porch and stood before the door. The windows on each side were boarded over. An ancient padlock, brown with rust, hung below the doorknob.

Jennifer stopped and sucked in her breath. She pointed to the door. It was already open! It was as if the lock was there only for looks.

"You're not scared are you?" Cass whispered over her shoulder.

Just crossing the porch had Jennifer's heart leaping in her chest. What would it be like to actually go inside? Jennifer's feet felt like stone.

"I'm too terrified to be scared," she answered. Taking hold of the knob, she pushed the door open and stepped inside.

CHAPTER 7 ✿ INSIDE!

Inside the house it was dark and still. Gloom was thick all around. It seemed to Jennifer as she stood in the doorway that the castle was holding its breath, waiting for something to happen. As she stepped forward, she immediately felt the presence of something else in the house. Could it be the ghost? Her mother had often commented on Jennifer's keen sixth sense. Right now she would gladly have traded it for a handful of courage.

Suddenly her flashlight flickered. The light died. Darkness closed in. Jennifer grabbed Cass and stifled a scream, waiting for something to leap out and grab them. But nothing happened. Nothing jumped out from the shadows. Nothing at all. Several seconds went by before Jennifer relaxed her grip on her friend.

"That was spooky," Jennifer said, shakily.

"Yeah," Cass agreed in a whisper. She squinted her eyes. "This must be the kitchen."

As their eyes adjusted to the dark, the girls could make out what had been the kitchen. There was a wood-burning range with a broken stovepipe, a sink full of leaves, and some shelves. The walls were blotched with stains, and there were holes where the plaster had chipped and fallen down, littering the floor.

No matter how softly they tried to walk, their footsteps echoed in the emptiness with alarming loudness as Cass led the way through the kitchen and into a long hallway.

Opening off the hall were rooms, bleak and bare. No furniture remained. The boarded-up windows were shrouded by veils of cobwebs. The air was stale and damp. Jennifer found it hard to breathe.

Groping their way along the hall, the two came to an archway. Moonlight filtering in narrow rays between the boards on the windows cast a purple hue, lighting up a large room with a high ceiling. Stripped of furnishings and carpets, only the tattered remains of curtains bordered the windows that stretched nearly to the ceiling. Jennifer could make out an empty picture frame on the wall. A single chandelier, its crystals dimmed by decades of dust, dangled like a forgotten star in the center of the room. Somewhere upstairs the wind rattled a shutter and whistled dismally down the chimney.

Disappointed at finding no fancy furniture, and certainly no treasure, Jennifer shifted her attention to the end of the room where a staircase, with carved banisters, wound up and up into the darkness of the house.

"Pssst. Watch me," Cass called, her voice bouncing around the room. She stood under the chandelier waltzing with an imaginary partner. Jennifer was imagining the room full of people laughing and dancing when suddenly her dream was shattered by a screech. A rumbling sound came from the backyard. The noise grew louder and louder, shaking the whole house.

Upstairs a door slammed and a dog yelped. "Sink yer teeth into me, will you!" a raspy voice shouted.

"It's the ghost!" screamed Cass. "Let's get out of here!"

There was nowhere to run as footsteps came pounding down the staircase. The girls dove into the far corner just as a figure, hidden in the darkness, rushed past chasing after a shadow. The noise thundered away and all was silent. Only the smell of cigar smoke lingered in the air.

Cass and Jennifer huddled in the corner, absolutely still with fright. "Let's get out of here now," urged Jennifer. She crawled forward.

Cass yanked her back. "Wait. Not through the kitchen. It still might be out there."

"Out a window then," Jennifer insisted. "But let's go now."

Cautious as cats, the girls crept toward a nearby window. They tugged furiously at the boards that crisscrossed the empty frame. A heavy plank came loose and rattled to the floor. Jennifer hoisted herself up, swinging her legs out the

window. Ducking her head, she dropped to the ground below. Cass crashed down in the bushes beside her, knocking into a cellar window.

As Cass rolled over, a long sad howl rose up from behind the glass. A ray of moonlight fell across a black face with yellow eyes and fangs. It snarled and lunged madly as if it would burst through the glass to get at them.

"Run!" Jennifer screamed and took off through the bushes.

Without a word, Cass followed. They crashed through the undergrowth along the side of the yard, keeping to the shadows, too terrified to look back in case some monster was in pursuit.

By the time they reached the gate, Jennifer's arms were scratched and bleeding, her jeans torn. Cass was first across the road. She flung herself over the bulkhead. "Hurry, Jennifer!"

Jennifer landed with a thud in the rocks and took off after Cass. The tide was going out now. Scrambling and slipping, the girls raced along the water's edge. Jennifer's breath came in quick hard gasps. Her legs felt wobbly and uncoordinated as she splashed through the tide pools after Cass.

"Come on!" Cass urged.

Jennifer's sides ached as she fought to keep up. Why had she listened to Cass? It was crazy to be sneaking around at night. She was done with the awful notion of ghosts and treasure. Done!

CHAPTER 8 ❧ POISON OAK

Even when Jennifer was safely under the covers with the windows shut and the bunkhouse door securely blocked by a brick, she had trouble sleeping. She tossed and turned, the skin on her neck prickling and burning. By morning, Jennifer's neck was covered in a blotchy rash that itched so badly she had to see the doctor.

"Poison oak," the doctor said after a close look. "Summer folks don't know what it is. Looks like a sort of oak tree only it's a bush with leaves that go red. Kind of like your neck, young lady."

She chuckled then handed Jennifer a tube. "Put this ointment on three times a day, and try not to scratch or you'll be spreading it all over."

"I wonder where you got into poison oak?" Mrs. Chang sighed as she turned the car into the driveway at the top of the hill. "And how did your arms get so scratched?"

Jennifer just shrugged. "Do I have to stay in bed, Mom?"

Mrs. Chang switched off the engine. "Afraid so, honey," she replied.

"Oh, Mom. Can't I please go over to Cass's house for a little while?" Jennifer desperately wanted to see Cass to make sure that all her memories of last night – the ghost, the strange rumbling sound, and the black face at the cellar window – really had happened.

"No, honey. You look tired. You rest in bed, and we'll see how your neck looks tomorrow."

Mrs. Chang and Jennifer started down the path. "What's wrong with her?" Margo shouted up the hill. "Is it contagious?"

"On second thought I think I will go lie down," Jennifer said. Peace and quiet sounded better than answering everyone's nosy questions.

There was nothing much to do in the bunkhouse. Jennifer had already decorated it to her satisfaction. It certainly did look better. The brass bars on the bed shone like gold when Jennifer polished them. Margo's curtains had added a cheerful touch, and the dresser, though somewhat old-fashioned, fitted perfectly.

Her eyes surveyed the walls. Beneath the array of animal posters, the board walls barely showed. Jennifer leaned against the dresser. She looked from one poster to the next, finally stopping on her favorite, which tacked above the bed. It was a picture of a dog show with people parading their dogs before a panel of judges. Jennifer walked over and studied it more closely. First came a tall skinny woman with hair like spaghetti walking an Afghan, next marched a plump man with jowls leading a bull terrier, and finally waltzed a lady with a head of frizzy pink hair leading an equally frizzy pink poodle. They both had their noses pointed high in the air.

Jennifer smiled. If I had a dog, she thought, it would not be tall and skinny or short or frizzy and definitely not pink. It would be the kind of dog that would wag its tail and come running when it saw me get off the school bus. It would chase sticks and go swimming, and it would be very brave. Jennifer imagined how nice it would be to have her own dog right now. It could sleep in the bunkhouse and go with her wherever she went. That would keep the ghost of Abel Bunratty miles away, she decided.

But who was she kidding? She didn't have a dog, and her chances for getting one seemed slim. Perhaps a summer in the bunkhouse would prove to her parents how responsible and self-reliant she was. Once they realized how grown-up she'd become, they definitely would allow her to have her own dog.

The thought cheered her up, even though the foul-smelling ointment was doing little to stop the itching on her neck. Jennifer hung her key necklace on a hook and decided a look through Isabelle's hatbox might help her feel better.

She got down on her hands and knees and slid the hatbox out from under the bed. She marveled at the size of it. It was nearly as big around as their barbecue grill. I wonder how big Isabelle's hats were? Jennifer thought to herself as she lifted the lid.

Before she could peek inside, the door opened. "Yuck. What stinks in here?" Margo, arms laden with magazines, kicked the door open wide and stepped in making sniffing noises. "It smells like your old socks crawled under the bed and died."

"It's not my socks," Jennifer retorted. "It's the medicine for my neck."

"You won't be bothered by any vampires, that's for sure," she said, making a face.

"Maybe it repels ghosts too," Jennifer said, hopefully.

Ignoring the comment, Margo dropped the magazines on the bed. "Here. I thought as long as you were cooped up you might like to look at my magazines."

Pictures of exhausted athletes covered in sweat didn't interest Jennifer very much. "Thanks, that's a nice idea," she said, trying to sound grateful.

Margo plopped down on the bed ruffling through the pages of a magazine. "There's a great article in here about using natural stuff to heal skin problems like sunburn and rashes. Nothing personal, of course, but I thought it might help you get rid of your plague or whatever that stuff you've got is."

"It's poison oak, not the plague."

"Sorry," Margo said, tossing the magazine aside. "What are you doing anyway?"

"I was going to see what's inside Isabelle's hatbox," Jennifer said and lifted the lid. The scent of lavender drifted out, and small puffs of dust rose through the room.

"Can I see those?" Margo asked, pointing to a bundle of photographs. They were tied together with a pink ribbon.

"They're really crumbly," Jennifer warned. The edges of the pictures fell apart in her hand as she passed them to her sister.

"Moldy oldies," Margo snickered and untied the ribbon. The photographs had been packed on some sort of rose-colored material wrapped in layers of tissue paper.

Jennifer stood up and shook out the fabric she'd discovered in the hatbox. A long dress, covered in sequins, unfolded to the floor. The high neck and loose waistline were like the dresses the women in Jennifer's history book were pictured wearing in the 1920s.

"Wow, check it out," cried Margo. "It's the same dress Isabelle's wearing in this picture."

"It is?" Jennifer looked over her sister's shoulder.

In the photograph, a young and beautiful Isabelle was standing in front of a stone sundial, her arm in the arm of a short but powerfully built man who was smoking a cigar. Unlike the pictures in the photo album, there were no other people in the background, and Isabelle was smiling.

"She sure is pretty when she smiles," Jennifer remarked.

"This must be her boyfriend," Margo said. She held up the next photo. "Look," she said. "Here they are again, sitting in a rowboat. Funny, there weren't nearly as many houses along the beach back then." Margo pulled out the last picture.

"This must be when they went on a picnic. Look at all the dogs. Aren't they gorgeous?"

Jennifer leaned over and looked at the photo with interest. There was Isabelle and the man with the cigar sitting on a blanket in the shade of a willow tree. They were in a park or a garden with rosebushes and fruit trees behind them. Isabelle was feeding a group of dogs something out of a basket. The man was laughing. Although the picture was happy, it gave Jennifer a vaguely uneasy feeling in the pit of her stomach.

"I wonder why this man isn't in any of the family-album pictures with Isabelle's aunt and uncle?" Jennifer asked.

"Maybe they had a fight," Margo suggested, handing the photos to her sister.

"They don't look like they'd ever fight about anything," Jennifer replied.

"Can I show that old dress to Mom?" Margo asked. "She'll get a kick out of it."

"Sure. Go ahead." Jennifer handed the old dress to her sister and sat down to take a closer look at the pictures. There was something about them that was bothering her, but she did not know what it was.

Margo waltzed over and held the dress up in front of the mirror.

"I'm so lovely. Oh, so lovely!" she began to sing at the top of her lungs as she swayed.

"Is Jennifer here?" Paul asked, peering curiously at Margo through the window, as she continued to sing, oblivious.

"Oh, uh, um..." Margo stammered, shoving the dress behind her back.

"I'm over here," Jennifer waved.

"Wow, you look almost as bad as Cass," Paul remarked, as he stepped inside. "She's got red bumps all over her arms. She's been moaning and groaning so loudly I thought you might have heard her."

"When we fell out the window!" Jennifer cried, suddenly realizing the poison oak must have been growing right where they landed when escaping from Bunratty's ghost.

"What did you say?" Margo asked.

"Oh, nothing," Jennifer sighed.

Paul looked at the photo Jennifer was holding nervously in her fingers. "Isn't that the lady who used to live in your house?"

"Yes, it is," said Margo. "That is Isabelle Adams herself."

"I wonder why on earth she's having her picture taken with that creep?" Paul asked, sitting down next to Jennifer.

"He doesn't look creepy to me," Margo remarked. "He looks very handsome, like a real gentleman."

"Who is he?" Jennifer wondered.

"Don't you know?" Paul laughed. "That handsome gentleman is old Abel Bunratty!"

"My gosh," cried Jennifer. "The ghost?"

"That's right," Paul said, flipping through the other photos. "And everything I've ever heard about him makes him sound crazy, crazy, crazy."

Paul glanced at his watch and stood up. "I have to go. It's time for my daily run."

"You run? How far?" asked Margo.

"Usually three or four miles a day. There's a perfect loop I discovered a few years back," Paul explained.

"What a coincidence," Margo said. "I love running too."

Paul raised his eyebrows. "You do? I haven't met many kids who like running. You want to go running with me today? I'll show you the cool running loop."

"Sure," Margo replied, tossing the dress on the bed. She followed Paul out the door. "Where's this great loop?"

Paul grinned. "You'll see – it's perfect," he said.

"Hey, and afterward I'll show you some soccer drills I just learned," Margo said.

"Great," Paul replied. "I've been in a rut lately. Oh, Jennifer," Paul said, reappearing at the door. "I almost forgot. This is for you."

He tossed a folded piece of paper on the bed and disappeared down the steps with Margo.

CHAPTER 9 🌹 THE NOTE

Before she opened it, Jennifer knew who the note was from. Not only was it folded, but the edges were sealed with tape. Feeling like a secret agent, she picked off the tape and unfolded the note.

Dear Jennifer,

Poison oak – what a drag. My arms itch like crazy! Your sister told my mom you had it too. Must have been growing under you know whose window. Did you know your sister comes over here all the time to bring my mom things she doesn't need? I know all she really wants to do is drag my brother out to kick the ball. He actually likes it. Weird! Anyway, my mom is making me stay home until Saturday. I feel as if I'll pop if I don't find out what that face at the window was. Let's make a deal. The first one to feel better goes down and looks in the cellar window again. If you agree, hang something red over your doorknob (on the outside, naturally). If the answer is no, then I'll know you really are a chicken. See ya later, alligator!

X X X
Cass

Jennifer's excitement from receiving the note faded at the prospect of another midnight trip. In her heart she knew there was no way she could ever bring herself to go out all alone at night. Especially if it meant returning to the castle. If she was captured by the ghost, there would be no one to help her. No one at all. Even if it meant the loss of Cass's friendship, Jennifer knew she could never do it.

Pushing the photographs aside, Jennifer kicked off her sandals and lay back on the bed. Fat Cat, who was now allowed to come and go as he pleased, jumped in through the window. After giving the hatbox a sniff, he leaped up on the bed. He put his paws on Jennifer's shoulder and purred in her ear. She stroked his head and started to think. So many strange things had happened to her after just five days on Vashon Island. Would the whole summer be this crazy?

Jennifer closed her eyes and tried not to think about any of it. But her mind kept coming back to the empty house, the ghostly feet pounding down the stairs, the strange howling, and the black face at the window.

With a heavy sigh, she rolled over and dozed off.

"It's good to see you back in the land of the living." Mrs. Chang smiled.

"It's good to be back," Jennifer replied, thinking nervously about her return to Bunratty Castle. "What's for dinner?" she asked, trying to get her mind off her fear. "I'm ravenous."

Margo tottered in from the kitchen balancing one of Mrs. Chang's colorful pottery bowls on a tray. A heap of fragrant vegetables lay steaming on a bed of rice.

"Health food," she beamed, setting the bowl in the center of the table.

"You made that?" gasped Jennifer. Margo liked to cook about as much as she liked to sew – especially food that was good for you.

"I sure did," Margo replied, pushing her chair up to the table. "I chopped vegetables and herbs all afternoon after Paul and I went to the vegetable stand in town."

"No more junk food for our favorite potato chip–powered athlete?" Mr. Chang asked as he spooned vegetables on his plate.

"Well, I guess vegetables and stuff aren't so bad," Margo confessed. "Anyway, Paul said his soccer game improved when he gave up chips and other junky stuff."

Jennifer piled some vegetables and rice on her plate. "I thought you didn't let anyone tell you what to eat?"

Margo grinned. "With Paul it's OK. He's been playing soccer for a year longer than I have, so he

might know something I don't. Anything's possible," she said, laughing.

"Well, anything to cut down on that huge potato-chip bill we're still trying to pay off," Mr. Chang laughed.

"Whatever I can do to help, Dad."

"You're starting to sound grown-up, Margo," Mr. Chang smiled. "Why don't we all finish the jigsaw puzzle together after dinner?"

But Mrs. Chang had promised to show Cass's mother how to make pottery bowls. And Paul and Margo were going to the first of the parks department beach fires at Burton, where they could roast marshmallows and hang out.

"How about it, kiddo?" Mr. Chang asked Jennifer. "Feel like helping your dear old dad with that puzzle? An extra set of hands is always a welcome addition!"

Jennifer happily agreed, and after the dinner dishes were washed and Margo and Mrs. Chang were gone, Jennifer started working on the puzzle out on the table by the front window. It was a dark night. Outside she could see only a few house lights flickering across the harbor at Dockton.

Mr. Chang sifted through the remaining pieces. But before he could find one that fit, a heavy thump sounded on the roof followed by a frantic scratching and then a bang.

Feet raced across the roof over Jennifer's head. She leaped up, her eyes wide with panic. "Something's on the roof, Dad!" she cried.

Just then there came a tapping at the window next to her. A masked face with beady eyes stared in. Jennifer screamed and ran to the kitchen. The creature followed around the porch and banged on the screen door.

Her father crossed to the kitchen door.

"Dad, don't open the door. Please, don't. It'll get me!"

"Calm down, Jennifer," Mr. Chang said. Slowly, he opened the door. On the other side of the screen, three masked faces peered up expectantly.

Jennifer blinked. "Raccoons!" she cried. "Only a family of raccoons." A flood of relief swept over her and she laughed. "They made enough noise to be a..."

"A ghost?" her father teased.

"Something like that," she replied and tossed a piece of lettuce out to the raccoons. The biggest one grabbed it and washed it in Fat Cat's water bowl.

Secretly Jennifer wished it was only a family of raccoons haunting Bunratty Castle. But she knew in her heart it was something much more sinister than that.

CHAPTER 10 ❀ FACE AT THE WINDOW

The next morning, Jennifer found her mother on the porch hard at work pressing the foot pedal on her pottery wheel. The wheel clicked with an even rhythm while her mother's hands began shaping a chunk of clay. As she held her hands firmly around the clay, it became round. By pressing her thumbs into the center as the wheel spun, Mrs. Chang made a hole and stretched it wide. Then, by cupping her hands and lifting the sides of the clay, it grew into a wide-mouthed vase. A look of concentration crossed her face as she pressed one finger along the upper edge of the vase forming a curved lip.

"That's a good one, Mom," Jennifer said as the wheel slowed. She loved to watch her mother making beautiful things on the wheel. It looked almost like magic.

Mrs. Chang looked pleased. "Thanks, honey." She wiped her hands on a towel and said, "Mrs. Krewson told me that there are lots of artists living on the island. They've got a co-op shop at the north end. I'm going to try to sell my pots there."

"That's a great idea," Jennifer agreed, proud of her mother's talent.

Mrs. Chang cut the vase from the wheel with a flat knife and set it on the railing. She looked at Jennifer's neck. "Your neck looks much better today. It's not nearly so red. I think I'll let you out of quarantine long enough to mail a letter for me down at Burton."

"OK," Jennifer nodded, following her mother into the kitchen. "Maybe Cass is better too. She can go with me."

"I wouldn't count on it," her mother replied, reaching for her purse. She handed Jennifer some change. "Mrs. Krewson wasn't very pleased with Cass's progress last night. She seems very protective of her daughter. By the way, what's that red towel doing hanging on your doorknob?"

"Oh, I'm just letting it dry out. Bye, Mom!" Jennifer tucked the letter in her pocket. The screen door slammed behind her, and she started walking down the path.

She looked up at Cass's window, but there was no red cloth in sight. Jennifer was disappointed, but she was glad to be out in the sunshine herself. Sunlight speckled the trees and slid in patches over the trail. It was a beautiful day.

When she reached the beach, Jennifer saw that the tide had gone out. Sandals off, she found a stretch of warm sand to walk on.

Looking down, Jennifer wondered what had made the hundreds of pencil-sized holes in the sand. She hadn't taken more than three steps when she found out. "Help!" she shrieked, as a blast of icy water came shooting out of the hole by her heel and trickled down her leg. She jumped aside in surprise as two more streams of water came jetting up from nearby holes. "What's down there?" she asked out loud. Getting down on her knees, she dug cautiously in the sand, uncovering one of the culprits.

"A clam," she laughed, lifting the spoon-sized shell out of the hole. Retracting its neck the clam squeezed its shell together tight. "Only a clam. I guess I really am a chicken to be scared by a clam!" Jennifer told herself.

She buried the clam and brushed the sand off her hands. The sun warmed her face as she began to walk.

After a while she went up to the logs that lined part of the shore. Washed up by winter storms, the logs were now bleached by the sea and sun and felt smooth under her toes. Wedged between two logs Jennifer spotted a piece of driftwood shaped like a wing. She sat down and pried it out.

She was just considering how good it would look above the fireplace, when her thoughts were interrupted by the sound of a boat smacking the surface of the water as it roared across the harbor.

Jennifer looked up to see a boat pulling a girl on skis. As the boat approached, Jennifer watched the girl crouch down over the waves, lean out, then shoot across the wake. Her hair blew straight back as she went flying up in the air making a fan of water behind her as she landed. She swung back like a pendulum, jumping the wake again.

The boat and skier flashed past. Jennifer watched. Impressed by the girl's skill and daring, she remembered how scared she'd been even wading in Quartermaster Harbor.

She rolled a rock over with her toe, sending a family of crabs scurrying for shelter. Jennifer shook her head. They didn't seem nearly as frightening now that she knew what they were.

Pulling on her sandals, Jennifer tucked the driftwood under her arm and started down the beach road. Although she did not cast so much as a glance at the houses lining the road, she knew when she passed by Bunratty Castle. Momentarily she was pierced by the feeling that the house, or someone in it, was watching her.

When she reached Burton, she bought a stamp at the post office and dropped the letter in the mailbox outside. She thought of calling Cass, but a plump woman with orange hair was already tucked inside the phone booth talking excitedly. Jennifer decided to wait. She sat down on the post office steps and drew a picture in the dust.

"Now see here, Louie," Jennifer heard the woman's voice rise to an angry wail, "two thousand dollars is a steal." The woman began shouting, "They are all in excellent condition. Every one of them a purebred too!"

Then, to Jennifer's amazement, the lady banged down the receiver. But instead of leaving, she immediately dropped more change in the phone and angrily dialed another number.

Tired of waiting, Jennifer bought a stick of beef jerky at the store and went back down to the beach. Already the tide had come in far enough to cover the sand. With the piece of driftwood under her arm, she walked back by the beach road, kicking a stone as she went.

Her promise to Cass began to nag at her as she walked. The very idea of visiting the strange old house by herself sent shivers up her back. Especially now that she had heard the ghost and seen that face in the window. Or was it only raccoons living inside? The face in the window – maybe. But the weird shadowy figure on the stairs – never!

In the corner of her eye she saw the gate. Its No Trespassing sign glared at her. Jennifer shaded her eyes as she looked up at the castle. In the morning light, and in the company of birds and flowers, the castle no longer seemed haunted, just lonesome and old. If only she could have a look now.

And why not? The note from Cass never mentioned when the first one who was well enough should have to go back to the castle. Jennifer thought how much easier it would be to see inside during the daylight. And safer too.

Without hesitation Jennifer set down the driftwood and stepped through the gate. She pushed her way through the tall grass. Stopping to unhook her shirt from a bramble, Jennifer's eyes caught sight of something like stone poking out from beneath a mound of morning glory vines.

Checking to see that no one had noticed her enter the yard, she crouched low and made her way to the center of the grounds. It was hard to tell what the stone was. At first she thought it might be a birdbath, but pulling away a handful of vines, Jennifer uncovered a flat surface of stone. She tugged away more vines and discovered the stone was round, like a tabletop set on a thick stone base. Moss covered most of it, but in several places Jennifer could see where Roman numerals had been carved into the stone.

It took Jennifer a moment to realize that it was not a birdbath or a statue, but a sundial. The *same* sundial in the photograph of Isabelle and Abel!

The feeling that time had come to a halt at Bunratty Castle sent a shiver of anticipation down Jennifer's spine as she turned to head toward the old house.

Picking her way through the brambles that snagged at her clothing, Jennifer skirted around into the high weeds at the side of the porch where she and Cass had made their escape two nights ago.

She froze, scarcely able to believe what she saw. The window from which she and Cass had leaped had two boards blocking the opening!

Who but the ghost of Abel Bunratty could have nailed boards back up so soon? Maybe it was all a dream. But the poison oak and the promise she'd made Cass were real enough.

Cautiously, Jennifer crawled through the tall grass. As she neared the cellar window, she hesitated at the sight of a stubby bush with red leaves. She stuck her tongue out at it. Then, she cautiously peered into the cellar window half expecting some ghoulish face to be looking back.

To Jennifer's relief, the cellar appeared empty. She rubbed a clean spot on the glass with her sleeve. The cellar was a square room with stone walls. Piles of old newspapers were stacked on the floor next to what looked like a heap of broken china. A lantern hung on a peg by the stairs on the opposite side of the room. Pushed into one corner was a bowl of water.

That's curious, thought Jennifer. What's the water for? Ghost dogs don't drink water, do they?

As if the thought had caught the attention of the ghost dog itself, a black shape scrambled out

from the shadows and leaped at the window, jumping and barking and falling back again.

Jennifer fell back ready to run when suddenly she realized what it was. A dog! It's a real live dog, trapped in the cellar!

The dog, black as night, stood beneath the window, pawing the wall and wagging its tail hopefully. Jennifer shoved a stick in the crack between the wall and window, prying it open an inch. As she did, a swarm of black puppies came bounding up and hid behind the mother dog.

"Aren't you beautiful," Jennifer whispered, trying to stick her hand in through the window. But the big dog, excited to see her, began howling a long mournful howl that was sure to alarm the neighbors.

"I'll be back," Jennifer promised. She dropped the stick of beef jerky through the window and then pushed it shut.

The dog's cry echoed sadly behind her as she raced across the yard toward home.

One mystery, at least, was solved.

CHAPTER 11 🌹 INTO THIN AIR

"This is crazy," Jennifer complained from her bed where she sat watching Cass open the back of her camera. Ever since Friday morning when Jennifer had told her friend about the dogs in the cellar, Cass had been eager to sneak back to investigate. Now it was Saturday evening and Cass was well enough to go to the beach fire at Burton. At least that's where the girls had told their parents they were going.

"It is not crazy. It is proof," Cass insisted. She dropped a roll of film in the camera and closed the back.

"But ghosts don't show up on film," argued Jennifer.

"Neither do ghost dogs," Cass agreed. "But real dogs will. And if we get a picture of them, they will have to believe us."

"You mean tell our parents?" Jennifer was horrified at the idea.

Cass stopped what she was doing. "Hmmm, I guess we would get in trouble."

"I guess so," Jennifer replied, pacing across the floor. "Sneaking out, trespassing, snooping around in someone's house. I'd be in trouble all right. I'd have to give up the bunkhouse, and I wouldn't be allowed to have a dog until I was ninety-three!" Jennifer never kept secrets from her parents, but she felt anxious at the thought of them ever finding out about this.

Cass sat down cross-legged on the floor, thinking. "I know," she spoke up. "We could mail the pictures and an anonymous letter explaining the whole thing."

"Who would we send them to?" Jennifer asked. She leaned against the dresser, nervously fiddling with the ruby earring on the shelf.

"I don't know. But we can't let those poor puppies starve in the cellar!" Cass insisted.

In her heart Jennifer knew Cass was right. She hadn't stopped thinking about the look on the black dog's face or the whimpering puppies trapped in the cellar at the mercy of Bunratty's ghost.

Jennifer set the earring back on the shelf. "Why do you suppose the ghost keeps real dogs?"

"Beats me," Cass shrugged. "Ask him next time you see him."

"Ha, ha. Very funny," Jennifer snorted. Suddenly, her eyes grew wide. "Hey, I know who we could send the pictures to."

Cass looked up. "Who?"

"To the Society for the Prevention of Cruelty to Animals. They're always rescuing animals from cruel owners."

"Does a ghost count?" Cass wondered.

"A ghost that keeps dogs locked in the cellar and chases them up and down the stairs counts as cruel in my book," Jennifer remarked firmly. Filled with a renewed sense of courage, she picked up the earring and dropped it in her pocket for luck. The rash on her neck no longer itched and only a few red bumps remained. She reached up and took the secret key necklace off the hook. Pulling it over her head, she tucked it inside her jacket.

"All set?" asked Cass, standing up.

"Let's go," Jennifer replied. "Oops." She stopped in her tracks.

"What's wrong now?"

"I forgot to get new flashlight batteries at the store," Jennifer sighed. "But wait. I've got a lighter." She pulled open a drawer and rummaged through the contents until her hand fell on a yellow butane lighter. She pulled it out. "It's to light a candle in case the electricity goes off."

Cass looked at the lighter skeptically. But before she could say anything, Margo opened the bunkhouse door. "Get it in gear, you two, or we'll be late for the beach fire. It's nearly eight thirty already, and Paul's already waiting for us down at the boat shed."

It was a hazy pink sunset. The boats on the harbor took on a purplish tinge as the sun slipped below the horizon. Jennifer and Cass tagged along a few paces behind Margo and Paul, who were passing a soccer ball back and forth between them.

Just as they reached the gate of Bunratty Castle, Cass stopped. "Hold on a minute, Paul. I've got a cramp in my leg. I'm going to sit down." She leaned on Jennifer and together they hobbled over to the bulkhead.

"Are you OK?" Paul asked. "We can walk slower."

"Oh, no. I'll be fine. You go ahead. We'll catch up in a while."

"You sure?" Margo asked.

"Sure I'm sure," Cass nodded. She sat down, pretending to look out at the water. A moment later Jennifer whispered, "They're gone. Let's get this over with."

The light was fading fast as the girls slipped through the gate and entered the tangle of weeds. Glowing orange in the last rays of the sun, the house looked especially forbidding.

They neared the cellar window. "Can I look first?" Cass asked, crawling ahead of Jennifer in the bushes alongside the porch.

"I don't hear anything," Cass continued, peering expectantly in the window. Her smile faded and she sank back on her heels. "I don't see anything either!"

"What?" cried Jennifer. Pushing her face up to the glass, she tapped lightly. No welcoming yip was heard. The cellar was still. The water dish was nowhere to be found.

"It's not what you think," Jennifer cried. "I know exactly what I saw and there was a black dog and six puppies. Honest!"

"Then where are they?" Cass asked. "What happened to them? A room full of dogs does not vanish into thin air unless..." Her voice trailed off.

"Unless what, Cass?"

"Unless the ghost of Abel Bunratty took revenge on them. Maybe he chased them up and down the stairs until they..."

At that moment from within the house, a sorrowful wail rose up, shattering the silence. Then a voice shrieked, "I'll get you after what you did to me. I'll get you!"

Somewhere a door banged shut. The voice died and the howling faded away. All was quiet.

The silence was more terrifying than the voice. "Let's go," Cass whispered. "We can come back tomorrow morning."

But a change had come over Jennifer. Her terror had turned into something else. Something she'd never felt before. Stronger than her fear of the ghost was her determination to save the dogs before it was too late.

Jennifer shook her head. "We can't go," she said firmly. "If Abel Bunratty is torturing those dogs, it's up to us to stop him – now."

"I think I liked you better as a chicken," Cass frowned. "But I guess you're right. Tomorrow might be too late."

Because the girls knew their way, they quickly slid in through the back door, which stood ajar as before, the rusted padlock in place. Again the feeling of another presence touched Jennifer like an icy finger.

They stood in the shadowy kitchen and looked around. "That must be the way to the cellar over here," Cass said, pointing to a door at the end of the kitchen.

Jennifer and Cass exchanged looks of apprehension. Her stomach in knots, her knees still shaking from the strange voice, Jennifer stepped up and grasped the doorknob firmly. At first the door was unwilling but, with a shove, it creaked open grudgingly.

Jennifer had fully expected to be greeted by the black dog and her puppies bouncing and yipping up the stairs. Instead there was silence. Only the musty odor of old papers rolled out the door. A solitary moth fluttered in the air of the empty cellar.

Bewildered, Jennifer followed a dusty shaft of moonlight down the steps into the cellar. At once the girls saw that the floor near the steps was littered with something white. The broken china,

Jennifer thought as she felt in her pocket for the lighter. Kneeling down, she flicked it on.

"Bones!" screamed Cass, turning her head aside. "We're too late. He got them."

Jennifer was too stunned to move. She shut her eyes against the sight of all the bones broken into pieces and scattered in piles across the floor.

"But we heard a dog only a few minutes ago," Jennifer argued. She forced herself to look again. "Cass," she said after a moment. "Don't these bones look a little big to be from dogs?"

Cass glanced down. Her face went white. "But Jennifer, if they're not dog bones, what are they from?" She edged back.

"I don't know, but I think we'd better look around upstairs."

Cass sighed and pulled Jennifer to her feet. "Now I know I liked you better as a chicken."

Creeping up the cellar stairs, the girls crossed the kitchen and started down the hallway looking for signs of the dogs. They found nothing.

Jennifer felt desperate. The dogs couldn't be dead. They had to be somewhere in the house.

It was just as they passed under the archway into the living room that Cass stopped and whispered, "Maybe he's got them up there."

Jennifer turned. Cass was pointing to the staircase that wound up four stories to the tower. There was no other place to look.

CHAPTER 12 🌹 THE TOP OF THE STAIRS

Inside her stomach Jennifer felt fear twisting itself into a knot as she and Cass started up the staircase. The wood banister, smooth under Jennifer's hand, led them up and up. The girls kept to one side in case the boards creaked, but no matter how lightly they moved, their steps seemed to echo up the passage.

Time after time they stopped, thinking they'd heard something, but each time it was the noise of their own footsteps. Jennifer was reminded once again of the presence of someone else in the castle.

After the first two flights of stairs, the air was getting dusty, and Jennifer's legs began to ache. She thought about turning around. Yet even to look back into the gap of darkness below made her feel as if she and Cass were in a nightmare where the ground floor had vanished, leaving them trapped on an endless flight of stairs spiraling up to nowhere.

All at once Jennifer wished she was safely at the campfire with Margo and Paul roasting marshmallows, talking with people, and having fun. She tightened her grip on the rail. Her heart thundered in her chest as they climbed up, getting

closer and closer to the top of the stairs. The thought of reaching the top terrified her even more.

Suddenly, a shadow swooped down, flapping at her head. It brushed against her cheek. Jennifer ducked and stifled a scream as her hands flew up to cover her face.

"A bat," Cass whispered, anxiously. "Keep going, quick, before he knows we're here."

There is nothing to be afraid of, Jennifer told herself. Absolutely nothing. But what if she opened the door at the top and it wasn't the dogs who leaped out?

For the first time, Jennifer felt like an intruder. Was the ghost of Abel Bunratty watching them already? Waiting? Ready to grab them by the ankles with his icy hands and hurtle them down the stairs like rag dolls? She tried desperately to erase the picture of his sinister form, racing down the staircase after the beautiful black dog and her pups.

Jennifer stopped and looked down four flights to the bottom floor. For once Cass didn't pester her to hurry. Perhaps her friend was filled with the same thoughts.

After what seemed an eternity, they reached the top. Before them stood the door. Jennifer glanced at Cass then felt for the knob. Was it her imagination or did it feel warm? Hardly daring to breathe, she turned it to the left, praying for it to be unlocked. It was. The door slid open with a creak. Jennifer waited. There was silence.

Stretching her head around, she peeked inside. "Oh, my gosh," she cried. "You're not going to believe this, Cass."

CHAPTER 13 ❧ THE TOWER

Never taking her eyes off the room, Jennifer pulled Cass in behind her and shut the door with a click.

"Wow," murmured Cass, her eyes trying to take it all in. "This is really weird."

For as much as the lower floors of Bunratty Castle were stripped bare and were gloomy with decay, the tower room was a palace. Moonlight came in through the lace curtains. Cass and Jennifer could see that the round room with a pointed roof was filled with elaborate furniture. It appeared well kept.

Two rocking chairs stood before a marble fireplace. The carpet was worn to threads under one of the chairs where someone had sat and rocked for many years. Long velvet curtains bordered windows that looked out over Quartermaster Harbor. Above each window was an arch of glass with a red rose in the center. On a table under one window, Jennifer could see two cups, their delicate patterns barely visible in the silvery light. A picture leaned up behind them. Overhead, a chandelier sparkled in the moonlight.

Jennifer ran her hand over the top of a wooden bench. The well-worn wood felt soft and silky. The scent of lavender, ever so slight, tickled something in her memory.

"Jennifer, come here. Feel this." Cass was kneeling before the fireplace, her hands stretched over the grate.

Jennifer blinked. "It's warm," she said. "And I smell tobacco." Jennifer looked around the room. "You know, Cass, I get the feeling that someone has been in here, and not so long ago. The fireplace is warm, there's not a trace of dust anywhere, and..."

"But that's impossible," Cass interrupted. "No one has even been inside Bunratty Castle for fifteen years!"

That same eerie feeling swept over Jennifer. Why would a room be left like this, full of fine old furniture and valuable things, when the rest of the house was in shambles? And why, Jennifer wondered, was the tower room so clean? Who used it? And more important, when did they come?

There was only one possible answer – the ghost of Abel Bunratty. That's who came to the tower room. It could be no one else.

Bewildered, Jennifer sank down in the chair behind her. How could a room that felt so warm and inviting be the haunt of a ghost? Her thoughts were interrupted as Cass gasped and pointed.

"That's it! That is the rocking chair where Abel Bunratty died and the dogs ate him. Don't sit there, Jennifer. Please don't."

Jennifer almost felt like laughing. To her the tower room felt like a haven compared to the rest of the lonely old house. She sat and rocked, letting her head fall back on the cushion. "What's in that?" she motioned to a box on the mantel.

"I'm not going to touch it," Cass said, shaking her head. "I'm not touching anything. I don't want the ghost of Abel Bunratty seeking revenge on me."

Jennifer pushed herself out of the chair. On the mantel she noticed the stub of a candle. Using her lighter she lit the wick, then lifted the lid of the small ivory box. A look of recognition crossed her face as she reached inside. "Look, Cass. It's the other one," she smiled, lifting something the size of a thimble from the box.

It glowed red in the candlelight as she held it up for Cass to see.

"The other ruby earring!" Cass cried, stepping closer. "What is it doing up here?"

"I don't know," Jennifer replied, dropping it in her pocket. "But I think we'd better take a closer look around."

It was hard to put into words, but despite her fears, despite the danger that surrounded her, Jennifer had the feeling she was about to discover something more than dogs or ghosts or hidden treasure. It was this intuitive feeling that compelled her to explore the tower room.

With Cass at her side, Jennifer circled the room holding the flame before them.

"Look there," said Cass, pointing to the table. "Isn't that the picture of Isabelle and Abel on their picnic?"

Jennifer picked up the fancy frame that held the photograph. It was old and blurry but definitely the same picture that was in Jennifer's album. The only difference was the writing in the lower corner. It was so faded it was nearly impossible to read under the flicker of candlelight.

"Can you tell what it says?" Cass asked, squinting her eyes at the spidery writing.

"Even though we can't have today," Jennifer read slowly, deciphering the scrawl, "there will always be tomorrow."

Cass shrugged. Her eyes met Jennifer's. "What is that supposed to mean?"

"I'm not sure," Jennifer replied, setting the picture down. "I'm not sure what any of this means, yet." Jennifer knew there had to be a simple answer. She believed the earrings, the photographs, the secret key, the revengeful ghost, the message on the picture, yes, even the disappearing dogs, were part of the mystery of Bunratty Castle. But the more Jennifer tried to figure it out, the less sense it made. It was as if the

pieces of different jigsaw puzzles had been mixed up together. There were too many pieces and no place to fit them.

"Oh, no. I don't believe it," Cass cried, looking up at the ceiling. "Tell me you see what I see."

Jennifer looked up. On a beam directly over her head, glimmering in the candlelight, hung a key. The girls exchanged looks of amazement.

"Here," Jennifer said, as she set the candle down. "Help me pull the rocker over. I think I can reach it if I stand on the armrests."

They positioned the chair under the beam. With Cass steadying the chair, Jennifer crawled up, stretching to her full height. As she reached for the key, she heard footsteps and instantly froze.

Thump... thump. Something was coming up the stairs! Thump... thump!

There it was again. Jennifer stood absolutely still, hardly daring to breathe, praying that whoever – or whatever – was coming up the stairs would turn around and go back down.

Yet the noise came closer and closer until it was just outside the door. It stopped. Then the doorknob began to turn.

"The ghost is coming!" screamed Cass. She let go of the rocker. The chair fell away and Jennifer tumbled to the floor.

The door flew open. Out of the darkness stepped a figure. Suddenly, a light shone in her face.

CHAPTER 14 ✿ THE GHOST

"Got you!" a raspy voice growled.

An arm shot out and Jennifer was pulled to her feet and pushed down in the chair.

"No!" Cass cried, backing toward the fireplace. "Leave her alone!"

Too terrified to move, Jennifer stared up through the blinding light to see not the face of a ghost, but a bearded man with narrow eyes glaring down at her. A cigar hung out of the corner of his mouth.

Frightened as she was, Jennifer shielded her eyes from the light. "Who, who are you?"

"I'm the big, bad ghost," the man snarled. Pulling the cigar from his mouth, he blew a cloud of sour-smelling smoke in the air.

Breathing hard, a heavy woman lumbered up the stairs and leaned against the door, her breath coming in strangled gasps.

The man grinned. "Looky here, Mabel. You were right!"

The woman, strangely familiar, heaved herself across the room. She studied Jennifer and then Cass, a grim look of satisfaction on her face.

"Ha, I knew someone had been foolin' with the windows. Didn't I tell you, Jack?"

106

"Sure did, Mabel," the man replied with a nod.

"Now that we got this pair of meddling little snoops here, what do you reckon we should do with 'em?"

Something in the woman's arms squirmed as she brushed a strand of orange hair out of her eyes. "I know what I'd like to do," she hissed. Bending over, she poked her nose in Jennifer's face. "I'd like to get rid of them!"

Suddenly, Jennifer recognized her voice. This was the same woman she had overheard in the phone booth in Burton on Thursday. A lump rose in her throat. She sat frozen, her mind wild with fear.

Jack looked at his watch. "All rounded up and loaded, Mabel? We got customers paying big bucks for these fancy mutts."

"They're ready," Mabel replied, shifting the whimpering bundle in her arms. "Drugged 'em up good this time so they won't be wiggling under the blankets. All except this one."

The big lady unfolded her arms and held out a black puppy. The puppy kicked its legs in the air. "This one's no good. Legs are crooked. Won't bring a good price. Can't afford to be feeding those expensive bones to a runt."

"Looks like the one that bit me, anyway," Jack snarled. "Give it another shot and let's get going." He looked hard at Jennifer. "What about these two snoops?"

Mabel examined the captives with cold eyes. "We'll leave 'em. Lock 'em in. Make it look like the bolt slipped. No one could hear 'em yelling from up here, and it's a four-story drop to the ground. When they finally do find 'em, they'll think they were vandals. Or maybe folks will think the ghost got 'em!" Mabel shook with laughter.

A slow, sly smile crossed Jack's face. "You're a real thinker, Mabel," he said.

Mabel held the puppy firmly under one arm while she extracted a hypodermic needle from a case in her pocket.

"What is that?" Jennifer asked.

"Just a little something to put this mangy mutt to sleep for good."

Sobs of fear clutched at Jennifer's throat. Her body tensed as she watched Mabel pinch the skin on the dog's neck, preparing to insert the needle. Jennifer tasted salt on her lips and knew that tears were rolling down her cheeks as she struggled with the fear that held her frozen. "No!" she cried, suddenly throwing herself out of the chair.

Surprised at her own courage, she pushed past Jack and wrestled the dog from Mabel's grasp.

"So, kid, you want to play rough do you?" Mabel sneered. She started toward Jennifer, waving the needle in her hand.

"Come on, Mabel," Jack interrupted, flinging his cigar butt in the fireplace. "We'll just make the last ferry to Seattle if we hurry."

Still laughing, Mabel turned and followed Jack, slamming the door behind them. Outside, the bolt clicked into place. The sound of footsteps echoed down the staircase.

Then the girls were alone, locked in the tower room with no one to help them and no way out. Jennifer didn't move until the roar of the engine faded away into the night.

"Oh, Jennifer," Cass sobbed from the corner. "We're trapped. We're going to die up here. We're going to die!"

It took Jennifer a minute to comprehend what had happened. A warm lick on her face from the dog brought her to her senses. For the first time she noticed her knee hurt. It throbbed where she must have hit it against the chair as she fell. The puppy whined, nuzzling its cold nose into Jennifer's neck. Reaching up to stroke it, she felt something clutched in her hand. It was the key.

"I must have grabbed it as I fell," she murmured.

"What?" Cass said, wiping away her tears.

"The key," Jennifer explained. "I must have grabbed it when I fell off the rocking chair."

Cass sighed deeply. She looked out the window. The lights of a single car sped along the road toward the ferry. "So what? You're looking at a key, and meanwhile we're stuck in this tower until someone happens to find us or we shrivel up and die like old Abel."

Jennifer cuddled the puppy, and it fell asleep in her arms. She glanced at the key. Suddenly, something in her mind clicked. Setting the puppy on the bench, she started for the door. A sharp pain shot through her knee and her legs wobbled beneath her.

"This is it, Cass," she cried, full of hope. "This is the key to the door. We're free!"

Cass grabbed the candle and held it as Jennifer brought Abel's key up to the lock. She pushed it one way and then the other way. She fumbled with the lock, but the key would not fit.

"Oh, no," Cass said, more disappointed than ever. "Why are there so many secret keys that don't open any doors?"

Jennifer's mind searched for an answer. She looked closely at the key under the candlelight. It looked remarkably like the key around her neck. Unhooking her necklace she held the keys next to each other.

"Well, I'll be a cross-eyed camel," Cass cried. "They're identical."

"Not quite," Jennifer said. "Look. The prongs on the end are different sizes."

"Well, go ahead. Try Isabelle's key," Cass said, crossing her fingers.

Jennifer held Isabelle's key up to the lock. Without any effort the key slid in and clicked. The tower door swung open.

They were free.

CHAPTER 15 ❀ POLICE

"Where have you two been?" demanded Margo, planting her hands on her hips. "Everyone has gone home already."

Jennifer, who was walking slowly because of her sore knee, and Cass neared the edge of the fire. Only a few coals still glowed orange and red under the starlit sky.

"Sorry," Jennifer apologized. "We were busy."

"Doing what?" Paul asked. "We were worried. We thought you'd been kidnapped."

Paul noticed something squirming under Jennifer's jacket. "What have you got there?"

Jennifer unzipped her jacket. A round head popped out and yipped.

"A puppy," cried Margo. "It's so cute. Can I hold it?"

"That's what we've been doing," Cass explained, hurriedly. "Someone... um," she began to falter.

"Someone moved away and left this puppy in a house, so we rescued it," Jennifer finished, passing the dog into her sister's outstretched arms.

Margo cradled the puppy to her chin. "You'd better not tell Mom and Dad you were poking around someone else's house," she remarked as the puppy licked her face.

Jennifer felt in her pockets. Aside from the earrings and Abel's key, they were empty.

"Cass, do you have any money?"

Cass checked her pockets. "This is all I've got," she said, pulling out the camera. "I guess I forgot I had it," she said, sheepishly.

Jennifer turned to her sister. "Margo, can I borrow some change for a phone call?"

"A phone call at this hour? Who are you calling?"

"It would take all night to explain," Jennifer said. "But you can hold the puppy while I'm gone."

"Oh, all right." Margo held the dog in one arm as she fished around in her pockets. She dropped some coins in her sister's hand. "Here you go."

"Be right back," Cass called as she and Jennifer climbed up the bank. Ahead, the bright light in the phone booth shone like a beacon in the street in front of the post office.

It was decided that, because her voice was deeper and sounded more mature, Cass would call the police to report Jack and Mabel. With Jennifer squeezed in the phone booth next to her, Cass dialed the emergency number and waited, listening for someone to answer. Then a voice crackled, "Vashon Police Department. Officer Kowalski speaking."

"Good evening, officer," Cass said, making her voice quaver like that of an elderly woman. "This is... this is... um," Cass stammered. "Ahhh, this is... Isabelle Adams... of Burton beach. I wish to report some suspicious events!"

Jennifer covered her mouth to stifle a laugh.

"You must be a summer person," Officer Kowalski remarked. "I don't recall your name on the voter register."

"That is correct."

"Now, what seems to be the problem?"

"Well," Cass continued, "the past few nights I have seen some people, one tall man with a beard and a large lady to be precise, sneaking in and out of Bunratty Castle with dogs!"

There was silence on the other end. "Are you sure?" Officer Kowalski asked. "It sounds as if you might have lost your marbles, madam."

Cass covered the receiver. "He doesn't believe me. He thinks I'm nuts."

"Keep talking," Jennifer insisted. "And whatever you do don't let him hang up."

"Now, look here, young man," Cass continued. "I am certainly not crazy. I know what I've seen."

"Uh, er," the policeman mumbled. "It could have been vandals."

"No. Those people are dognappers, I'm sure of it. I saw them load their car with pedigree dogs – they were going to be sold in the city!"

114

Cass heard papers being shuffled on the other end of the phone. "Say, you might have something at that," the police officer remarked. "We've had a pile of stolen dog reports these past six months, including a collie, two poodles, and a black Labrador about to have puppies. Those people could be dognappers. Give me a description of that car."

"I can't," Cass stammered. "That is, there is no time. The thieves are heading for the Seattle ferry right now."

"The last ferry goes in twelve minutes!" the officer exclaimed. "I've got to contact the squad car immediately."

Cass dropped the phone on the hook and let out a nervous sigh.

"You did it, Cass. You were terrific!" Jennifer said, patting her friend on the back.

Just as they stepped out of the phone booth, a pair of headlights blazed around the corner and a police car shot past, speeding toward the ferry dock.

"Hey you two, hurry up," Margo called from the beach. "It's almost ten o'clock. You don't want to get into trouble do you?"

"Not us," Jennifer giggled back.

Margo gently put the sleepy puppy back into Jennifer's arms, then, kicking the soccer ball to Paul, started down the road toward home. Jennifer tucked the tiny dog inside her jacket and zipped it partway up so the pup could sniff at the night air.

Jennifer and Cass, following several paces behind, walked in thoughtful silence. The moon above cast a soft light along the road. Both girls turned to look at Bunratty Castle as they passed by. With the mystery unraveled, all the terror, all the intrigue, had gone out of the place. It stood peacefully, like all the other houses on Burton beach, washed in silver light.

Jennifer felt neither happy nor sad. For her, the spirit of Bunratty Castle would never fade away. She knew the mystery had come to an end, and with it, the adventure. It had been wonderful, though: meeting Cass, sneaking out, exploring the castle, and rescuing the dogs. There were probably hundreds of kids who grew up safe and secure

116

who never tasted the fear or felt the excitement she and Cass had.

Jennifer's thoughts were interrupted by the touch of Cass's hand on her arm. "You're not going to tell your parents what happened are you? Are you?"

It was the same question Jennifer was asking herself. She imagined how upset her parents would be if they did learn what she and Cass had been up to. She knew, also, how awful she'd feel if she lied. After all, hadn't she already been brave enough to go sneaking out at night, brave enough to enter a haunted castle, brave enough even to outwit two dangerous dognappers? But was she brave enough to confront her parents with the truth about what had happened?

Jennifer hugged the puppy to her chest and felt that same spark of courage still burning within her. "Cass," she said softly, "I am going to tell them."

Cass's eyes bulged with surprise. "But won't they be furious? Won't they make you give up the bunkhouse? Won't they make you share a room with Margo?"

"Probably," Jennifer had to agree.

"And what about the puppy? They'll never let you keep it if you tell them what we did. Never. I think it would be much easier to stick to the story about someone moving and leaving the dog."

Jennifer nodded. "I know it would be easier, but I'd never feel right about helping catch those dognappers if I lied." Jennifer kicked a stick out of the road and continued. "Cass, I've never lied to my parents. They trust me. And that's more important to me than the bunkhouse, or even keeping the puppy."

Jennifer fully expected Cass to be mad. It was obvious that if she explained the whole story to her own parents, Cass would have to confess to her mother as well.

"Oh, well," Cass said, running her hand through her hair. "I'd probably talk in my sleep and blab the whole story anyway." She gave Jennifer a friendly punch in the arm.

"You know what?" Cass said, as they neared the paths that led up to their homes. "I'm sorry I ever called you a chicken. The way you insisted on going into the castle, stood up to Jack and Mabel, and want to tell your folks the real story, well..." She paused to smile, "I think you're pretty brave, for a city kid, anyway."

Jennifer smiled back. "Thanks, Cass. And good luck with your mom."

"You too. See ya later, alligator."

"After a while, crocodile!"

CHAPTER 16 🌹 ISABELLE'S SECRET

The next afternoon Jennifer was sitting on the edge of the bed gazing thoughtfully down at the small leather-bound book in her hands. The puppy lay sleeping in her lap, paws twitching as he slept.

As the bunkhouse door creaked open, Jennifer looked up. A hand, waving a newspaper, appeared. "Is it safe to come in?" Cass asked, peering around the door. "You're still alive?"

Jennifer grinned. "Yep. Alive and kicking. Come on in."

Cass sat cross-legged on the floor by the bed and looked at Jennifer curiously. "Well? What did your parents say when you told them about Bunratty Castle?"

"It's funny," Jennifer began. "I thought they'd go through the roof. But they didn't. They told me how awful they'd feel if anything happened to me, and how I could come to them if I had a problem. Then they lectured me on trespassing, and then do you know what they said?"

"That you were restricted to the house for the rest of your life," Cass said in an adult tone.

Jennifer shook her head. "They said they were proud of me for what I did. Then they said if it was all right with the owners, I could keep the puppy! I named him Abe, short for Abel."

"Parents are so weird," Cass said, shaking her head. "My mom yelled and said she'd ground me for life if I ever went sneaking out again. Then she said I couldn't go farther than our beach for a whole month. And then she hugged me." Cass looked at Jennifer and paused. "My mom hasn't hugged me since I was little. I thought she was going to cry. Heck, I thought I was going to cry! I guess I never realized how much she really loved me."

Cass's eyes brightened. "Hey, I almost forgot. Have you seen this?" She held up the island newspaper.

"Not yet. I've been reading something else," Jennifer replied.

"Well, take a look!" Cass spread the front page across Jennifer's knees.

"Oh, my gosh. I don't believe it!" gasped Jennifer, her eyes scanning the paper. The article began with a bold headline:

GOSSIPING GHOST GETS DOGNAPPERS

Local authorities report it was the ghost of Isabelle Adams who gave police information leading to the arrest of Jack and Mabel Magilicutty late last night at the ferry wharf. Police believe the two to be head of a large ring of dognappers in the area.

When questioned about the ghost, Officer Kowalski said, "I thought she was very polite. She sounded like a real person."

Jennifer laughed so loud she awakened the puppy. It crawled out from under the paper and tugged playfully at Cass's hair.

"Isn't that the most amazing thing you've ever read?" Cass giggled, rubbing the puppy's ears.

"To tell you the truth, Cass, there is only *one* thing more amazing than that."

"What could be better than all those people believing I was the ghost of Isabelle Adams?"

"This." Jennifer handed the leather-bound book to Cass, who looked puzzled.

"What's so great about an old address book covered in mold?"

"It's not an address book, Cass. It's a diary."

"Whose?"

"Isabelle Adams's," Jennifer exclaimed. "I found it on the beam right above the spot where I found the key to the tower."

"Oh, wow!" Cass said, opening the book. "Have you read it? What did it say? Did she talk about her boyfriend Abel?"

"Her husband, you mean!"

Cass looked surprised. "They were married?"

Jennifer nodded. "But secretly, because Isabelle lived with her aunt and uncle who wouldn't allow her to marry a common carpenter like Abel Bunratty."

"So they must have had secret keys to each other's homes. That's why the key we found in the bunkhouse got us out of the tower," said Cass.

"That's what Isabelle wrote in her diary," Jennifer agreed. "And I tried the key we found in the tower in the bunkhouse lock: it fits. She used to sneak down and spend time in the tower with her husband. Those ruby earrings were her wedding present from Abel."

"How romantic," Cass sighed. "But couldn't she have come out in the open with it after her aunt and uncle died?"

"I suppose she could have," Jennifer replied. "But Isabelle died first. She caught pneumonia and died in 1931. She was only twenty-eight years old."

"Poor Abel," Cass said. "He must have missed her a lot."

"Enough to live like a hermit," Jennifer agreed.

Cass frowned. "You know, Jennifer, I don't believe those stories about him chasing the dogs up and down the stairs at all now," she said firmly.

Jennifer agreed. "They're probably just exaggerated stories from snoopy neighbors. I'll bet the dogs got into the tower room, Isabelle and Abel's special room once, and Abel chased them out. That's all."

"I bet you're right," Cass replied, leafing through the pages of the diary. "And those dogs were probably his only company all those years."

"Sad isn't it?" Cass said. She closed the book in her hands and sat quietly.

Jennifer leaned back on the bed. Her eyes moved to the ruby earrings sitting on the dresser. To Jennifer these were more valuable than a whole chest full of treasure. She wouldn't sell them for anything. She'd keep them to remind her of Abel and Isabelle and their stolen moments together. She realized now that there was more to love than just words you said to someone. Love was something special. It gave you courage. Courage to do things you never believed you could do before.

Jennifer smiled thoughtfully. "After all this time, I like to imagine that Isabelle and Abel still meet up in the tower room with no one to disturb them, don't you think?"

"Absolutely. That's a perfect way to think about them," Cass agreed, happily picturing the scene in her mind.

Jennifer scooped up the wiggly black puppy and set him gently on the floor. "Bunratty Castle will be around for a long time. I'd like to go back up to the tower someday," she said, watching Abe chew on the corner of the rug and then pounce on a dust bunny. "What about you? Do you want to go back?"

"Someday," Cass replied with a mysterious grin on her face. "But right now I'd like to go take another look at the treasure map carved in the wood on the floor of the boat shed. If we can figure it out, we'll be millionaires!"

"Oh, Cass, you're kidding me," Jennifer said. "There isn't really a treasure map carved in the floor, is there?"

"Maybe," Cass replied with a grin. "Maybe not. There's only one way to find out if it's real or not. Let's go!"

FROM THE AUTHOR

I spent my childhood summers on Vashon Island. My parents bought a waterfront cabin there that was built in 1906. The old cabin looked in need of paint and repair, but to me it was the most beautiful house in the world. Just down the beach stood a grand old Victorian house with a tall tower. My friends and I always wondered what strange things could happen there. We made up ghost stories and were sure we could hear spooky sounds coming from that house at night. That's where the idea for *The Secret of Bunratty Castle* came from! The characters in the book are fictional, but many of the places are real and some of the events really did happen.

Lucky me! my husband, Richard, our son, Sam, and I now live full-time at Burton beach. We are settled in a big warm house at the top of the hill.

Marcia Vaughan

FROM THE ILLUSTRATOR

For as long as I can remember, I've wanted to be an artist. When I was growing up, my parents were constantly giving me encouragement and allowed me to pursue my interest in art. After graduating from high school, I went to the American Academy of Art in Chicago, where I built on my initial foundation of art education.

Through years of hard work and literally hundreds of fun and challenging assignments, I've managed to create a fulfilling life for myself in an exciting and ever-changing business.

As an artist, I feel the need to be constantly working. Even when I'm not involved in a particular project, I find myself in my studio painting, drawing, or sculpting. It's a great way to live, and I couldn't imagine it any other way!

Jeff Busch

That's a Laugh

Queen of the Bean
Cinderfella's Big Night
The Flying Pig and the Daredevil Dog
Ants Aren't Antisocial
Charlotte's Web Page
Playing with Words

Thrills and Spills

Mountain Bike Mania
Destination Disaster
Journey to the New World
The Secret of Bunratty Castle
Happy Accidents!
The Chocolate Flier

Challenges and Choices

Call of the Selkie
Trailblazers!
The Hole in the Hill
The Good, the Bad,
    and Everything Else
On the Edge
The Willow Pattern

Our Wild World

Isn't It Cool? Discovering Antarctica
    and the Arctic
The Horse, of Course
Trapped by a Teacher
Mystery Bay
The Rain Forest
Feathery Fables

© Text by **Marcia Vaughan**
Illustrated by **Jeff Busch**
Edited by **Alison Auch**
Designed by **Karen Baxa Hoglund**

© 1999 Shortland Publications, Inc.
All rights reserved. No part of this publication may be reproduced or
transmitted in any form or by any means, electronic or mechanical, including
photocopying, recording, taping, or any information storage and retrieval
system, without permission in writing from the publisher.

04 03 02 01 00
10 9 8 7 6 5 4 3 2

Distributed in the United States by
    RIGBY
    a division of Reed Elsevier Inc.
    P.O. Box 797
    Crystal Lake, IL 60039-0797

Printed in Hong Kong.
ISBN: 0-7699-0421-1